IDENTITY

by

Nat Burns

Bella
BOOKS

2012

Bella Books, Inc.
P.O. Box 10543
Tallahassee, FL 32302

Printed in the United States of America on acid-free paper
First published 2012

Editor: Medora MacDougall
Cover Designer: Judith Fellows

ISBN 13: 978-1-59493-281-6
33614080829509

Other Bella Books by Nat Burns

House of Cards

The Quality of Blue

Two Weeks in August

Acknowledgment

Many thanks to editor Medora MacDougall for keeping my facts and words in line. And thanks to Carol, who listened to endless plot ideas and to Chris, who read numerous versions of the manuscript. I also want to thank my Aunt Jean and my sister Valinda—they've always been in my corner.

I'd like to dedicate this book to dog lovers everywhere. You are unique and fascinating individuals.

About the Author

Nat Burns' past work experience has included:
-Ten years as a staff reporter (with three Virginia Press Association Awards)
-Three years in tourism promotion as a media coordinator in Virginia
-Five years in technical support for a software development company
-Five years as the editorial systems coordinator for a Washington DC publishing firm.
-Teaching and supporting in local school systems
-Serving on the boards of Literacy Volunteers of America, Nelson County Education Foundation, Golden Crown Literary Society and SPWAO.

Nat lives in New Mexico, writing and editing full time. Bella Books has released five of her novels and has three more under contract. Nat is a book reviewer and is the music editor for Lesbian News, writing a monthly column called "Notes from Nat". www.natburns.com.

CHAPTER ONE

Sunlight was playing peek-a-boo along the top of Kerry Ridge when Eliza Hughes decided she'd had just about enough peace and quiet for one day. She peered into the white fiberglass cooler resting next to her and studied the mass of wildly thrashing small-mouthed bass. They eyed her accusingly.

"I know, I know," she sighed. "I'll let you loose in a minute."

She stood slowly, arching her back and stretching. She'd been sitting in this one place for hours, woolgathering as much as fishing, and her muscles had stiffened. It had been a beautiful afternoon though. She loved to sit, still as a statue, and watch as nature moved busily around her. The splendor of a black-speckled, red-eyed loon had captivated her for more than an hour as he complacently munched on baitfish.

She turned her attention back to the cooler of bass. "You guys will never learn, no matter how many times I tell you. It's a hook in there. Nothing that comes that easy is without a price. Get it?"

She reeled in and wrapped the fishing filament around her pole with an expertise born from years of practice. After wiping wet hands on her bib overalls, she hummed idly to herself as she moved to cross the narrow dirt lane to stow the pole in the white pickup she'd parked on the other side of Dooley Drive.

Without warning a moving mass of woman slammed into her. The pole went flying away and she tumbled backward. She didn't see where her pole landed, but she ended up sprawled in cold water with fish spewing from the tipped-over cooler.

"Holy crap!" a husky voice cried out, and suddenly Liza was looking into the largest, richest blue eyes she'd ever seen. "Oh my gosh, are you all right?"

Liza hated to pull her gaze away but glanced around at the wildly flopping fish and pondered her physical condition. There was a dull ache where she'd slammed into the cooler, but besides being wet through her midsection and legs and smelling a little like a pond, she was okay.

"Yeah, I think so," she answered. "The fish, though, we gotta get them back into the water."

Liza carefully extricated herself from the spill and reached to grab a handful of bass. The fish thrashed from her grasp and she lost her balance anew, falling onto the now muddy earth and soiling her entire right side. She glanced up, embarrassed, and saw that the woman was laughing at her. Liza rested there longer than intended as the woman's appearance washed over her.

Too thin, and fragile as dandelion fluff, the woman captured an onlooker's attention by the huge number of pastel freckles that dotted her unusual paleness. Her skin had the smooth texture of white alabaster, and the sun slanting against it made her glow with blue radiance. The glow was framed by a thick shock of auburn hair, pulled back into a ponytail but with strands escaping to frolic around her lean face. She smelled like coconuts. The scent filled Liza's senses, bringing them acutely awake. The woman's uncontrolled laughter finally penetrated and stirred Liza back to the matter at hand.

"The fish!" she muttered, scrambling to her feet. "Can you help me get them into the pond?"

Some of the fish had already flopped themselves to the bank and into the water with soft splashes. The others were totally beached, gulping air that provided them no oxygen, and they needed human intervention. The redhead set her MP3 player and phone aside and moved to help Liza. She promptly slipped and landed on her bottom in the middle of the growing mud bath of fish and water. Blushing, but laughing easily, the woman leaned to rescue the fish with her hands and toss them into the pond. Liza, on her knees, followed suit, scooping fish into both hands and ladling them toward the water.

The redhead's laugh was infectious. Soon Liza joined in, laughing even harder when she slipped again and fell backward, the two fish she was holding falling onto her chest and beating at her face with frantic paintbrush tails. The smaller woman plucked the fish from Liza's chest and struggled to her feet. She staggered to the bank, the fish jumping in her arms like popcorn in a popcorn maker. Knocked off balance by the effort of catching the uncooperative fish, she stepped too close to the edge and within moments had disappeared from Liza's sight.

"Oh no," Liza said, scrambling to her feet and carefully making her way to the edge.

The redhead sat in shallow water that reached to her shoulders and to the top of her bent knees. Dark rust-red hair, littered with pondweed, swept across and obscured most of her features. As Liza watched, she spat muddy vegetation from her mouth and uttered a groan of disgust.

The scene was too much for Liza. She laughed so hard her sides ached, the laughter issuing from her in huge guffaws. This lasted for almost a full minute before she could compose herself. With gasping breaths, she knelt and leaned forward, offering her hand.

"Here, let me...help you out," she gurgled, trying to catch her breath.

She glanced at the smaller woman and was surprised to see that the smiling blue eyes had changed into dark, swirling thunderclouds. The sweetly curved lips had pressed into a thin, stressed line. The woman ignored Liza's hand, cold blue eyes glaring at Liza amid the miasma of anger that surrounded her.

"Whoa, now," Liza began. "I'm sorry, but I didn't..."

The woman stood, sweeping the thick mane of hair from her face. Water raced from her sagging shorts and sweatshirt in small rivers. She wriggled her arms, trying to shake off the heavy water.

"Just move," she said, stumbling toward the bank.

Liza stood back and felt coldness rush across her. This woman was fierce.

"Look, hon," she began, spreading her hands helplessly.

"I am not your 'hon,'" the woman snapped. "My name is Shay. Now move."

Liza stepped back, daunted by the woman's meanness. "What I'm trying to tell you is, you can't get up that bank there without some help. It's steep and the roots twist all the wrong way. Hymie Clark stayed in there the better part of two days and a night until someone came along to help him out."

Shay seemed to finally understand Liza's words. She turned slowly and studied the banks of the large pond. Liza followed her gaze with her own. The pond, called Dooley's Folly, was steeply concave all the way around the shallows, the water level several feet below an overhanging ledge. The water Shay stood in wasn't but a few feet deep, but Liza knew that several hundred feet out toward the middle the depth was considerably more. Trying the other side would be fruitless, as the banks there were just as concave.

"Well, that's just crazy," Shay muttered as if to herself.

Liza nodded sympathetically. "I know. It's southern Alabama, though. There's lots of crazy here."

Shay was getting attitude again. "Just get me out of here," she said angrily, her voice harsh.

Liza felt devilment fly and took a good step back. She studied the frowning face, noting again how tan freckles peppered the long pale planes of her cheeks. She smiled mischievously.

As she watched Liza, Shay's face lit with alarm. Liza felt satisfaction stir.

"Say 'please,'" she said, studying her victim.

The words had a far different effect than Liza had imagined. Shay's body stiffened and if fire could have emanated from her eyes and ears, it would have. Liza didn't think she'd ever seen anyone as angry.

"Why, you ungrateful country bumpkin! How dare you!"

Her voice was just one octave shy of a shriek.

Liza bristled. "Who're you calling a bumpkin? At least I have more sense than to fall in Dooley's Folly!"

"Fall in? I was trying to help you with those damned fish. What the hell were they doing there anyway?"

"I just..." Liza didn't know what to say and certainly didn't want to say it to this prickly pear. "I just fish, okay? It's a hobby."

"Hobby?!" Shay spat. "Whoever heard...most people catch fish for sustenance, not play."

Liza opened her mouth to object but did not want to go there with Shay. Instead, she moved to the bank and held out her hand. "Let's get you out of my pond. You're polluting the fish."

Shay's mouth fell open in indignation, but she grasped Liza's hand and allowed her to pull her up the bank. As soon as she attained terra firma, however, she stomped off, her running garb clinging to her small form like a new wrinkled skin. Remembering her electronics, she turned with a scowl and retrieved them.

"You could thank me, you know," Liza called after her. Shay's only response was to swing one arm wide, sending a glistening arc of water into the late afternoon sunlight as she disappeared along the wide drive leading to the old Carson home.

"Crazy Yankee," Liza muttered as she surveyed the mess she had to make right. The cooler was muddy, but she knew she could hose that down at home. All the fish had made it into the pond, thankfully.

She pressed her booted foot into a puddle, folding soft loamy soil into the wetness, trying to even it out. She straightened a patch of sawgrass and spied her fishing pole. It was okay, a good thing as it was her favorite, a custom-made one crafted to be shorter than most standard poles. Liza frowned and looked along the path that Shay had taken. There was no sign of the woman.

"Good thing, too. She better not come back here with that bad temper," she told herself aloud.

Looking around, Liza pieced together the event that had triggered the muddy disaster of her afternoon. Shay had no doubt been jogging along the dirt shoulder surrounding the pond when Liza mindlessly stepped into her path.

After settling the pole and the cooler into the bed of her truck, Liza sighed and rubbed her sore shoulders. Who would have thought such a skinny gal could make that much of an impact?

CHAPTER TWO

Shay pulled the key from the back door lock and stepped into the mudroom of her home. She turned and patiently engaged the two slide locks and two deadbolts on the heavy steel door. She let a low shriek escape as she stomped through the dining room of her house, trailing water behind on the shiny wooden floor, and angrily flicked on every light switch she encountered.

Imagine the nerve of that woman.

"'Say please,'" she mimicked, screwing her fine features into a heavy scowl. Another light blossomed ahead of her. She should have known better than to move to this backwater hick town anyway. She should have stayed in DC where she belonged.

At the bedroom door, she switched on the overhead light, then paused and let her clothing fall from her body to pile into a sopping pyramid around her feet. Kicking loose from them, she stomped naked across the carpeted floor of the bedroom and into the bathroom. She turned the shower knobs harder than necessary and felt her anger ease somewhat as the heated stream flowed across her body.

Later, hair in a towel and face subdued, she scooped the wet clothing from the floor and made her way to the laundry room at the northern end of the house. She paused before entering the small, twilight-darkened room, sudden fear snatching at her heart.

"'Say please,'" she whispered as she reached around the doorframe to snap on the blessedly bright light.

The phone rang just after she switched on the washing machine. Rushing into the kitchen, she snatched her cell off the table and checked the caller ID. She answered it eagerly.

Shay sighed with pleasure. "Dee, how are you? You didn't call this afternoon."

Donald Sloan had been her best friend since he'd rescued her that sorry morning in October four years ago. They talked several times a day, and Shay had been worried because he hadn't called all afternoon. Her irrational fear that he had forgotten about her had spurred the run that resulted in her encounter with that horrible woman.

"I am so good. You've just got to meet him." His self-satisfied voice resounded in her ears.

"Him? Him who? Have you met someone?" Shay leaned into the refrigerator searching for iced tea. Finding the mostly empty pitcher she poured what remained into a glass.

"His name is Gregory, and we met at the law library. He asked for my phone number and I got his too."

"Aw, Don, I'm so happy for you. When will you see him again?" She took a long gulp of the tea, sorry that there wasn't more of it. Her run and the subsequent dunk in the pond had made her thirsty.

"This weekend. We're thinking about driving into the country, maybe doing some antiquing."

"That sounds like a great idea. Wish I could go."

"Now, Shay, I tried to talk you out of moving to that godforsaken place. My only hope is that you'll come to your senses and move back here with your friends where you belong. How was it today?"

"It was good. Strange thing happened this afternoon, though. I was out running, really getting into it, forgetting all about Pepper, and I run right into this gorgeous blond tomboy. I knocked her over and into this cooler of fish she had."

"Fish?"

"Yeah, she was fishing. Go figure. Anyway, there we were, in the mud, rescuing the fish by tossing them back into this pond." The corners of Shay's mouth lifted in unexpected merriment as she remembered the scene.

"And then what happened?" His voice was low and filled with curiosity.

"I was trying to carry some fish but slipped and fell, into the water, and of course, lost my temper, as usual."

"As usual," he echoed cheerfully.

"Then she started acting all bossy and it sort of scared me."

"Like Pepper?"

"Yes, like her."

"So then what did you do?" Real concern tinged his voice and she felt guilty for upsetting him yet again.

"Like I said, lost my temper, called her some rude names…"

"And beat a hasty retreat?"

Shay laughed. "Absolutely. How well you know me."

"Shay…you should have stayed and dealt with it. Not let her put you off that way. Not all women hit. Most don't. You know this. Until you can stay and deal with confrontation, you'll never get over all this crap."

Shay felt irritation stir. "I know, Dee. I seem to have no control over my reactions, though. My body is conditioned to react negatively even if my mind deems a situation okay."

Both sighed simultaneously, as if knowing some things couldn't be changed.

"I guess you haven't had a chance to tell Doc Frye about this latest…but what does she say to do about the fear you still have?"

Shay walked to the window and looked out at the forest thicket behind the house, thinking again that she should clear the land to improve visibility all the way around her property.

"I'm not seeing her anymore. Or anyone else."

"Then you've made up your mind."

Shay could hear his disapproval. She nodded, then realized that wouldn't translate across the phone. "Yes, I need to do this myself. It's not good to depend on a therapist the rest of your life."

Don laughed. "Hell, I'm putting my therapist's kids through college. I thought everyone had lifelong help."

"Well, that may be, but I don't feel good about it. I'm getting stronger every day. I should be able to deal with this."

"I wish you the best, sweetie. You know I'm on your side. Whatever I can do to help, let me know. I'm a good listener too. I should charge the same fees therapists do."

Shay laughed. Dee was such a dear friend. She thought of his comfortable job managing a branch of Regional Funds Bank. "You have more money than you can spend already. I don't think you need any more."

"Lifestyles of the rich and famous—a beer, a pizza and old Judy Garland movies until two in the morning. Hmmm."

"Whiner. What about this new hunk? This Gregory what's-his-name?"

Don fell silent and his voice changed, became more serious. "Who knows? I'm always willing to take a chance though. Here's Donnie boy, let's use him and stomp him a good one when we're through."

Shay replied quickly, disturbed by Don's pessimism. "He may be the keeper, honey. Trust your instincts. You're wise enough now to realize when you're being used that way."

"I hope so." He sighed deeply. "He's just so gorgeous, and I know I'll want to give him whatever he wants."

"Maybe he won't ask. What does he do?"

"Legal. Working as a lawyer. Just started with that big firm over on L Street."

Shay smiled and turned from the window. Her eyes scanned the bright front room, looking for shadows. "There, see. He'll have his own money."

"Yeah, that was part of the appeal. As soon as I saw his card, I fell in love." He laughed and Shay joined in.

"You are such a pain. Go do something banky. I'm going to unpack the china boxes and fill up Mother's china cabinet."

"Okay, but remember. She's in jail, Shay. Jail. Bars, butchy matrons, the whole nine yards. She's probably loving it. You can relax and enjoy life a little."

"I will. I know. Love you, honey. Thanks for being my friend."

"My pleasure, you know that. Hey, watch out for those gorgeous tomboys, though. I hear they're in season out there in the country, so they may be looking for shelter."

"You are so full of it," Shay replied, laughing.

After signing off, Shay scrounged yesterday's tuna salad from the refrigerator and made herself a sandwich. Eating alone at the small, wooden table, she glanced around her silent kitchen and felt a sense of gloom approach. She didn't like spending all her time alone but knew it would be a long time before she would be able to trust and allow someone to enter her life. The thought saddened her.

The death of her parents, so close together, had taken its toll, leaving Shay with a huge void in her life. And since her time with Pepper, Shay had lost touch with most of her established friendships, personal and business. Being a victim of abuse sometimes brings out a latent fear in people; Shay had seen it in several friends' eyes when the court case had become public knowledge. Now she faced the task of building a new life for herself in an entirely new town. She sighed and chewed. The task seemed so overwhelming; she wasn't even able to focus on it for any length of time.

Shay longed to be who she had been before Pepper entered her life.

Pepper. Dorothy Presley Pope: a handsome, muscular butch with white blond hair and dynamic blue eyes. She had a sweet smile too, one so sweet that it easily melted a woman's heart. It certainly had melted Shay's heart. Even now, when Shay pictured that practiced smile in her mind, her knees grew weak. The other images more than made up for that sudden lapse into weakness, however: the drunken rogue, the weeping penitent, the angry harridan.

Shay sighed and finished her sandwich. Fish. Fishing. She thought of the tall tomboy then and pictured her in her mind. What she could remember. Mostly she remembered perfect white teeth in a tanned face and strange eyes the color of pale coffee. She'd never seen eyes quite that color before. The color helped make the eyes more expressive, the *café au lait* mirroring the rapidly changing emotions Shay's behavior had engendered in her. Embarrassment and remorse nagged at Shay, and she vowed to apologize if their paths ever crossed again.

CHAPTER THREE

The house Liza shared with her father and her younger brother, Richard, was modest in appearance but rich in location. Situated at the edge of the Bon Secour National Wildlife Refuge, the aged, rambling home occupied a prime piece of real estate. Developers wanting to buy him out for the oil rights had already approached her father many times. Liza knew how much he loved it, though, and was sure he would never sell. This was part of the reason why, when he had been diagnosed with skin cancer and was preparing to undergo treatment, he'd called Liza home from the outskirts of Montgomery, to care for him and also, she was sure, to help jump-start her love of the old home place.

The second born of Tom and Sienna Hughes' four children, Liza knew she was the most dependable. The oldest, Steve, successfully sold insurance for a living but drank more than a little and wore a belligerent attitude as though it were a three-piece suit. His wife, Mary, an old school chum of Liza's, complained constantly, and Liza had listened to way more grief about her brother than she cared to admit. Two good things had come from their stormy marriage and Liza adored them. Her nephew, Mason, was a very mature ten, and her niece, Stevie, six, was a bundle of charm and manipulation.

Liza's younger sister, Chloe, was a Type A dynamo. If the theory of birth order flip-flopping was true, then Chloe was the poster child. Bypassing both Steve and Liza in ambition, she worked as a legal assistant, controlling the offices of Warren and Warren better than if she were a senior partner. Nothing happened in that office without her stamp of approval and both elder and younger Warren repeatedly sang her praises. Clearly, they relished her hypercontrol, which allowed them to go freely about the business of representing clients and bringing in the money.

The youngest child, their brother Rich, would forever be the baby of the family. It seemed he hadn't matured a lick since their mother died almost five years ago. Her death had been rough on him, and now, at age twenty-two, he'd yet to deal with the loss effectively and move forward. He worked as a cook at the local wings and beer pub and seemingly wanted nothing further out of life.

Entering the house, Liza paused to press a kiss to her father's forehead. He sat in his favorite easy chair watching a sports channel. This last round of focused chemotherapy had left him shrunken somehow. Gone was the overlarge, overloud man Liza remembered from her childhood. She still admired the hell out of him, however, as he was handling the fight against his illness with a grace and stoicism she found fascinating.

"Any calls, Pop?"

Tom looked at her with some confusion. "Are you expecting any?" he asked, his voice concerned.

Liza laughed and picked up the mail from the hall table situated just off the living room and rifled through it. "Damn, Pop, make a girl feel needed, why dont'cha?"

Tom laughed, realizing how his innocent question could be misconstrued. "Sorry, Baby Gal. No, no calls."

"Shoot. I was hoping Hector would call me with the stats so I wouldn't have to call the office myself. It's always so uncomfortable when she answers."

Tom fingered the remote, muting the patter of the announcers. "I thought Estella told you Gina wasn't usually in the office after three o'clock."

Liza studied a white envelope with the return address of Meadows Produce in Montgomery. She sighed. Another check. Money in the bank just didn't replace a good relationship. "I know, Pop. It's the one saving grace. I guess I'll go call, even though," she re-entered the room, glancing at her watch, "it's cutting it a little close."

"Well, what happened to you?" Tom asked, finally noticing her mud-coated clothing. "You're going to ruin the rug."

Liza looked down at the ancient braided rug that covered the pocked wooden floor. It had been in the house as long as she could remember and looked like it.

"Pop, come on," she said, making a face. "This rug?"

Tom had the grace to look embarrassed. "What did you do, catch the fish with your hands?"

"No, it was a traffic accident, sort of. Fisherwoman versus jogger. Jogger won, I think." She looked down at her overalls. "I guess I'd better go clean myself up. Hey, the jogger was a woman living at the old Carson place. Have you heard anything about someone moving in up there?"

Tom studied Liza's face, his mind obviously whirring as he gave her question a good amount of thought. "Seems like Bernie Cohen said something about a new woman in town. Said she was a looker."

Liza scowled. "Bitch, you mean. She's ornerier than a water moccasin." She paused in thought, looking much as her father had looked while thinking. "I guess she looks okay. A redhead."

Her father just grunted, his interest having shifted back to the game, so she made her way down the hall to her bedroom. She'd wait another hour or so before calling Meadows. Maybe Gina would have left by then for sure.

In her room, Liza loosened her coveralls and placed them in the hamper just inside the bathroom door. She'd wash them later tonight before the stain set in too well. Alabama soil this low in the Gulf was sandy and heavy with white clay. It often left stains in fabric. She also removed her socks and boots, leaving them on the tile floor. Her T-shirt joined her overalls in the hamper and she switched on the shower.

The heat felt good. She stretched her left side under the stream to expand and warm the muscles that had been hit when she'd fallen on the cooler. Looking down she saw that a bruise had already begun to darken along the side where the edge of the cooler had caught her.

Her mind drifted to the woman. Shay. She remembered how she'd felt upon first seeing her, when she was lying there in the mud, fish flopping all around. Her hands idly soaped her body as she remembered their time together and how the wet clothing had hugged Shay's delicate curves. She wondered what she had done to set her so on edge.

Liza shoved her head under the water, rinsing shampoo from her thick blond hair. She probably hated her and never wanted to see her again. Liza grinned into the stream of water. She seemed to be having that effect on just about all women these days.

CHAPTER FOUR

Odd. There was a dim light shining in her office. Who would be in the office at this hour? It was too early for the cleaning crew and besides, they usually had every light blazing while they worked. Jim William, at the front desk, should have warned her she had a visitor. Jim was responsible for noting the after-hours coming and going of the employees and patients in the Health Network building. She'd stood by his desk for several minutes too, shaking the wet snow off her umbrella into his waste can. They'd even made small talk, for goodness' sake! She paused in the hallway, uncertain. She shrugged off her fear. This building was about as secure as a building could be. Obviously, it must be someone approved by Jim or he would never have allowed the person inside.

The doctor moved slowly toward the door, keys in hand. The keys were unnecessary. The door was open, gaping several inches wide. Instead of wisely backing away and calling for help, Dr. Rachel Frye leaned her weight against the door, pressing it open with no sound. Gingerly she stepped inside, tiptoeing so her heels wouldn't tap on the tile entryway. It seemed there was no one inside at first, and then she saw the man. He was short, his long dark hair streaked with gray, and he was wearing a dark blue flannel shirt over tan trousers and hiking boots. As Dr. Frye watched, the man cursed softly and opened yet another drawer.

"Hey there, what are you doing? This is my office and you can't be in here." Dr. Frye's indignant tone was automatic, a knee-jerk reaction to the violation she felt. She switched on the overhead lights. The fellow looked up and fixed her with bright blue eyes set in a scarred, gaunt face.

"Where do you keep them," he asked, his voice rough and urgent, a slight foreign accent evident. "The patient files?"

"What files? You need to leave. Now!" She moved toward the telephone, peering closely at the intruder, trying to remember if he was a patient. If so, it might be something she could handle by herself.

"Who are you? Are you a patient? I don't think I recognize you…" He was older than she'd originally thought.

"The files," he repeated, moving toward her. Though short, he was sturdy in build and no less menacing than a taller person. "The patient records, where are they?"

Dr. Frye suddenly realized anew the possible danger. She moved back a step and stiffened her spine, unwilling to show her fear. She lifted the handset, certain now that she needed help.

The powerful man moved with eel-like grace through the room and was on her before she had a chance to complete dialing the front desk. As she fell, she thought about her gentle, helpless husband Lawrence. He'd be lost without her. As would her patients. Unable to catch her breath as the man's hands closed about her throat, she stared into his eyes with sudden recognition as the light dimmed around her. Sorrow filled her; sorrow for herself and for those she was leaving behind.

The assailant stood above her, chest heaving with exertion. His gaze was hard and dispassionate. He looked at his hands as if amazed that they could so easily crush a neck. After a moment, he resumed his methodical search of the office, finally grabbing up the woman's briefcase which had fallen, from her lifeless hands, to the floor.

CHAPTER FIVE

Placide's Place was like a second home to Liza. She'd visited often with her mother, coming several times a week to the large house overlooking Dooley's Folly to visit her grandmother, *la Mémé*, Rosaries Hinto, and to eat cucumber and cream cheese sandwiches washed down with sugary hot tea. As Liza approached the wide side door today, striding along the narrow, pocked sidewalk, she inhaled the familiar perfume of wild roses and touched their laden, swaying branches.

The tall, two-story home was fashioned of ruddy, locally created brick supported by eight-foot-long, twelve-inch-square beams of paisley-patterned black locust. It had been built when the area had been covered by ancient trees that had to fall before a home could be built. Sturdy panels of this wood made up the thick, iron-hinged doors as well. Liza, as a child, had spent much precious playtime battling to swing open their heaviness.

Inside the house, more of this wood, shiny from years of polishing, adorned the walls and most interior surfaces. When younger, Liza had fantasized that she was on a great ship, a cramped sailing vessel, trapped on a windless sea. Her grandmother's minimalist attitude and sparse decorating style had inadvertently fueled this fantasy.

This hilly, rugged section of Maypearl was one of the oldest in the area. While most of rural Maypearl featured pine thicket and scrub growth in the sandy, poor soil, this area was more like cooler northern climes, with towering deciduous trees such as elms, oaks, dogwoods and beautiful crape myrtles and even some evergreen trees such as ficus and holly. Coming here was much like entering another world, one that an older Liza cherished now more than ever before.

She found her *Mémé* in the solarium, planting lemon basil plants into long wooden window boxes.

Spying Liza, her grandmother rose and brushed her hands on the long apron she habitually donned each day.

"*Eliza, bon bebe, comment allez-vous?*" She pulled Liza into a gentle embrace.

"*Bon, et tu?*"

"*Bien, veritable.*"

Liza laughed. Clearly, her grandmother knew why she was there. "You'd better say you're okay. Chloe called yesterday and said you've been feeling poorly. What's going on?"

Rosaries shrugged, "*Le c'est les goutte.*"

Liza frowned. "*Les goutte? Je ne comprends pas.* Speak English, Grandmother."

Mémé frowned at Liza but complied. "The gout. Pain in the foot," she said in a heavily accented patois. "You know I have no patience with the English."

Liza laughed. "And you know Pop sure doesn't speak French at home. I'm so out of practice." She sobered. "Is it still hurting?"

"*Non*, it eases."

"You know it's what you eat, don't you? All that shrimp."

"*Crevette?* How you mean the shrimps?" She studied her

granddaughter with a smile dancing about her lips. Liza, as usual, wondered if *Mémé* was playing with her, pretending ignorance.

"Too much shrimp or meat makes the gout worse. You need to stay away from seafood until it gets better." She smiled sympathetically. "I know that'll be hard for you."

"Yes, the shrimp is my favorite," Rosaries agreed. "It will be hard but I will try less of it. The doctor says this too so I must listen. Enough of the pain. Come now and tell me about the family."

Liza held her grandmother's arm close as they moved into her cozy, well-lighted kitchen.

Placide's Place had been built by Liza's maternal great-grandfather, Renoi Boulanger, in the late 1800s after moving from Canada to the lower forty-eight. After his death, the house had passed down to his only daughter, Rosaries. She and her husband, Chayton Hinto, had shared it for more than forty years.

The era of its construction and the subsequent years had given the house a worn elegance. Though built in the Deep South, it was laid out very differently from most Southern homes, which featured wide-open spaces. Placide's Place, probably because it was built by a warmth-seeking French-Canadian, had small rooms that led one into the other or playfully skirted a logical connection. When young, Liza had delighted in losing herself in the confusing passageways and intriguing crawlspaces. She would then call out until Papa Chayton, a pure-blood Dakota Indian, would come find her. After guiding her into a main hallway, he would fold his arms and study her as if seeking answers, looking every bit the stereotypical cigar-store decoration. Liza would simply laugh and hug his legs, for his dark, leathery skin and long black hair was incongruous against his modern tie-dyed T-shirts and denim shorts.

The kitchen was the largest of the original rooms and served as the heart of the home. It offered a huge hearth, the fireplace rigged with iron hooks for cooking in stewpots. The room had been modernized around this hearth, but upon first glance, a visitor easily could be thrust back into the nineteenth century. During family gatherings, everyone gravitated here, mostly during mealtimes, ignoring the more formal dining room less than twenty feet away. The scarred oak table was the site of many heart-to-hearts, especially as Liza dealt with the loss of her mother, Sienna, Rosaries' beloved only child.

As *Mémé* busied herself with filling the teakettle, Liza settled at the table and let her mind reminisce about those days and the talks that had been her salvation during that difficult time. The loss of Papa Chayton just months later had cast a five-year pall on the entire family.

"Where are you going to put the window boxes?"

Mémé shrugged. "They're for the solarium because that plant smells so good. But for no place in fact."

"Particular." Liza's correction was so automatic that neither woman noted it.

She glanced out the large window next to the table. From this vantage point, she could see the tree-shrouded roof of the Carson house. Her thoughts flew to Shay and their strange encounter.

"Hey, *Mémé*. Have you met the people who moved in over at Carson's?"

"Hmm?" Rosaries lit the gas flame under the kettle and took a seat across from her granddaughter.

"*Carson place. Qui est-ce qui habiter?*"

"*Pas que je sache.* There's a mystery there." She shrugged. "From the...Blue?...this man comes and he say he looking for property."

They sat for some time in companionable silence, both looking out the window.

Rosaries answered the call of the singing kettle and filled two cups before resuming her seat and her conversation. "He say he looking for private place, no persons close. Wants to know if that house so. I say yes."

"So, what did he say then?"

"No more. He walk for a long time, then drive the car away."

"Then the woman moved in?"

Rosaries carefully sipped her tea and nodded. "*Oui.* Young girl with the flame hair."

"A redhead. Her name is Shay."

"Ah, you know this woman." Rosaries nodded sagely.

"Well, not exactly. I met her once. Let's just say I'm curious about her."

"*Curiosité tué les chat*," Rosaries responded.

"*Mémé*!" Liza retorted. "There's nothing wrong with some healthy curiosity."

Rosaries laughed. And, aware of and accepting Liza's predilection toward women, she never missed an opportunity to tease her about it. "Especially if *la femme* is beautiful. This one is very beautiful."

Liza's sense of humor took over. "I don't know, *Mémé*. She is a redhead and you know what they say about redheads."

Rosaries looked confused. "No, what is it someone says?"

"Well, it's common knowledge," she began slowly, "only two things are necessary to keep a redhead happy. One is to let her think she is having her own way, and the other is…to let her have it."

It took a moment for Rosaries to comprehend the joke, but once she understood, she chuckled into her teacup and shook an index finger at her granddaughter.

CHAPTER SIX

At last. Shay studied the long sheaf of paper in her hand and marveled at how heavy the thick pages felt. She looked at the note from George Madison, her lawyer back in DC. *Sign these,* he had written, *and you'll be rid of me finally.*

"And rid of his fees," Shay said aloud to the empty dining room. She looked out the French doors, once again marveling at how bright southern Alabama was. And the sun kissed the earth all year long here, not just for the four months or so she'd enjoyed in DC. Although widely separated from friends and professional acquaintances, Shay decided she liked living here. The sunlight and quiet sultriness of the surrounding bayous spoke to her somhow. She was grateful to have had the funds to escape to this new and different world.

The fight to bring Pepper to justice had cost a good portion of the inheritance left to her upon the death of her father four years ago, but overall, it had been worth it. Pepper, sentenced to five years for assault with intent to commit bodily harm, would not bother her for some time. Buying this house under an alias and through an international broker had been just one more step toward her escape.

Her thoughts flew back to the first time she'd seen Pepper. Club Techno 12-34 had been smoky that night, but even so, Pepper's neon blue eyes had captured Shay in a tractor beam of amused desire. Pepper moved toward her, the approach slow and meandering as she stopped to converse with friends along the way. She'd glanced at Shay now and again while smiling and laughing with her friends, as if making sure her target remained stationary. Shay hadn't moved, although her heart beat heavy in her chest as she imagined Pepper's hands on her.

Gaining Shay's side, Pepper had laughed a low, smoky chuckle of victory. She had known the effect she had on women. During the trial her more secretive predatory habits came to light, and Shay had been shocked anew that she was only one of the many who had fallen prey to Pepper's special charm.

An abrupt memory of struggling for comfort in a locked, cramped closet flashed into her mind. The vision shifted and she saw Pepper lowering her muscular, naked body onto yet another blond woman she had picked up over on Dupont Circle. They were usually palely blond and always small in stature. It was as though Pepper needed women smaller than she was to reinforce her power over them. Shay had watched them through the slatted door, God help her, unable to stop, noting how the pastel blond of both their heads blended so well. Pepper had turned to look at her many times during the lovemaking session, those blue eyes making sure that Shay was watching, that Shay had not escaped somehow, that she was still in Pepper's control.

Later would come the beatings...for imagined slights...for thoughts Shay had never entertained. And Pepper had infiltrated herself into every aspect of Shay's life, turning friends away and alienating business clients with her tactless behavior.

Sudden remembered pain in her fingertips caused Shay to

clench her hands into protective fists. There was nothing quite like the singular, exquisite pain caused by clawing a door until your fingernails pulled loose from the nail beds. How many hours had she lain in that closet, beaten and terrified into submission, abandoned by Pepper, the house dark and cold?

Shay sighed and laid the papers on the dining table. She looked at her new fingernails sadly. Someday Pepper would be free and might find Shay, no matter what precautions she had employed. Her one hope was that Pepper would be dispirited by her time in jail and would not seek out more trouble for herself. Maybe she would forget Shay existed and they could both get on with their separate, peaceful lives.

Shay feared Pepper. She also feared her own reaction upon seeing Pepper again. Would she be drawn in just as she had before? Would she find the woman just as irresistible?

CHAPTER SEVEN

"Well, there is one woman," Liza said quietly.

Rosemary's ears perked like an overwrought Lhasa apso. "Oh really. Tell me more."

Liza blushed. "There's nothing to tell. I only met her once, but I can't stop thinking about her."

Rosemary King, Liza's friend since sharing mischief in Mrs. Stone's freshman class, studied her closely. This was an unusual admission from her usually taciturn *compadre*.

"That says a lot, you know," she said finally.

Liza sighed and tapped the serving spoon she was holding against the rim of the metal chafing dish. It made a gentle, soothing noise.

Rosemary moved away to load a baked potato for Sly Cash. She winked at the elderly man. "Hey, Sly, how's tricks?"

Sly, who'd been homeless the four years that Liza had worked at the mission, shared a wide, gap-toothed grin. "Sure good, Miss Rosemary. No rain. The creek ain't rising. Guess that's about enough for me."

"Well, I'm glad to hear that," Rosemary responded. "You want some of these green beans? Liza here grows them and they're some of the finest in Alabama."

Liza laughed and nudged Rosemary. "Don't pay her no mind, Sly. She's just trying for an extra fine Christmas present this year."

Sly cackled spontaneously, almost upsetting his tray. Recovering awkwardly, he nodded assent to the beans. "Yes, indeed. I remember them as being mighty fine."

"He's fallen off," Liza whispered to Rosemary after Sly had moved along the line. She watched as he accepted a glass of iced tea from young Sarah Wellesly, a college student who volunteered two days a week. "Has he been sick?"

"I think it's just the booze taking its toll. Getting Sly to the doctor…well…let's say he'd have to be unconscious."

"But Doc comes every Monday," Liza argued. "Sly won't even see him?"

Doctor Clayton King, Maypearl's general practitioner, who volunteered at the mission, was like a beloved uncle. He was Andy Griffith, for goodness' sake! Liza couldn't believe he intimidated Sly.

Rosemary pressed her lips together into a line of negation as she placed a sloppy joe sandwich on a homeless woman's plate. "Nope."

Rosemary paused and examined the woman more closely. "Hello, welcome to New Life. I'm Rosemary and this is Liza. I don't think we've met you yet."

The woman smiled and Liza saw she was missing two teeth on the left-hand side. The large gap gave her smile a rakish air. She tucked her head as if self-conscious about the lack. "I'm Christine. Me and Tommy come down from North Carolina this week." She indicated the obviously inebriated man next to her in line. He was unshaven, rail thin and missing more teeth than his companion. He wore a battered watch cap over his long, wispy salt-and-pepper hair.

"Looking to stay warm, huh?" Rosemary studied the two with a practiced eye. She could ferret out troublemakers right away. Usually, if she suspected active substance abuse, she'd make them sober up before coming in. These two seemed harmless enough, although Tommy had definitely had a snort or two.

Christine nodded. "That's right. It gets cold up there this time of year." Her voice had a distinct North Carolina twang.

"I remember it well," Liza offered.

"Are you from there?" Christine asked, studying Liza with a spark of interest.

"I was for a while as a kid. Notice I'm back here now."

"Well, let me tell you all there is to tell about the mission. Mealtimes are posted on the door as you come in. We generally serve for about an hour. There are beds through that door," Rosemary added, pointing. "Men sleep on the left, women and children on the right. The bathrooms are at the end of this hall. There are hot showers and clean towels. Nothing fancy, just the basics. You need to remember that we don't allow alcohol or drugs or sleeping in the same bed and it's a firm rule. And if you smoke cigarettes, there's a porch out back. Make sure you use the sand bins we have out there; there's plenty of them."

She paused and took a deep breath, pondering what she had forgotten. "Oh, yes, if you have any pets, let me know and we'll make arrangements for them. If you need anything else you just let me or one of the other workers know; we'll take care of it."

"That sounds just about right," Christine said quietly. She smiled shyly. "Thank y'all so much for bein' here to help."

"We're happy to do it." Rosemary returned Christine's smile, then turned to fill Tommy's plate. Liza placed a generous scoop of green beans on Christine's plate, and with an extra nod of gratitude from Tommy, they moved on.

Liza looked at Rosemary. "You've got the rules and regs down to a science don't you?" She laughed. "I wonder how many times you've said those words over the past few years."

Rosemary wiped her hands on the skirt of her apron. "Too many, as far as I'm concerned." She paused thoughtfully and studied the room. "Then again, maybe not enough."

Liza palmed Ro's shoulder in understanding, then took

advantage of the lull to fetch more baked potatoes from the kitchen. She paused just inside, once again admiring the shiny industrial stove and oven that had been installed just a month earlier. Rosemary and her partner Kim Gilbert had worked like fiends to raise the funds so they could replace the ancient, half-functioning unit they'd had there before. Hector Thayer, of the BP gas station on Esperanza, had been a huge contributor as had Dr. King's wife, Paula, who ran the local florist shop. They had agreed to donate ten percent of each day's receipts for an entire month. At the end of that month, they'd raised enough for the mission to buy this electric beauty as well as the warming counter out front and some new blankets for the cots. Liza sighed to herself. Now if only they could get all the other businesses in Maypearl to follow suit, they could build a new, entirely separate mission.

She looked around. Actually, the basement of Recognition Baptist wasn't such a bad location. It was centrally located, was warm, had carpeting on the floor and great bathroom and shower facilities. It was a real blessing for the homeless of Maypearl.

"You daydreamin', Liza?"

Gloria Ebbe, Maypearl's head librarian and one of several mission volunteers, was eyeing Liza while holding up a large serving spoon expectantly. She'd entered from the back storeroom and caught Liza woolgathering. When Liza didn't answer right away, she moved toward the stove and used the spoon to stir a pot of simmering turnip greens.

"These cooked up tender," she commented, letting Liza off the hook.

Liza sighed and smiled. "They were young and grown in the cool. I had some the other night with butter and salt."

"Mmm." Gloria smiled. "Best bring me some to take home when you get a chance."

"That I will, sweet thing."

Liza hoisted a stainless steel bin of hot, foil-wrapped potatoes and stepped back into the serving area. The line was queuing up again so she quickly dumped the potatoes into the warming tray and moved on to peer at the other offerings. Everything was fine except the greens so she slipped back into the kitchen and brought out the heavy pan that Gloria had prepared.

Making her way back, she was gratified to see that the small dining room was almost full. She knew Rosemary harbored the worry that many of the town's homeless weren't being cared for, especially the mentally ill. Liza believed that they *were* cared for, the direct result of Rosemary's worry and hard work. The town wasn't that big. It was an old argument, though, and no one, not even her partner Kim, could convince Rosemary she'd done enough.

Liza studied the dining room with its hodgepodge of donated tables and chairs. When Liza first started helping out, right after returning to Maypearl from Montgomery, she'd assumed there would be an air of desolation among the homeless. She had expected that, because of their status in life, they would feel they were less than. She found the exact opposite to be true. The homeless were a hardy lot, used to innovation and creatively mastering difficulty in all its myriad forms. Unless mentally ill and delusional, they were usually proud of their rebellious lives, proud that they could beat "the man" at his own game. Work nine to five? Bah. Live the American dream with a Cape Cod and white picket fence? Bah.

One homeless man, Bobman Davies, who had passed through about a year ago, told Liza that he really didn't believe God meant for a man to limit himself to tending one little acre of land and doing that only. "Why else was there so much more out there?" he'd asked her.

"I mean we're hunters and gatherers from prehistory on," he'd explained. "It's only been in the last few centuries that man has settled in one place and started screwing up the world. I don't want no part of that."

Liza remembered his thoughtful, gaunt face and still had a world of respect for him. Her opinion was different, however. She wasn't stricken with the same wanderlust. She *liked* having her little plot of land to tend. She couldn't imagine not having a home, a place that was significantly hers.

She'd also seen the way the homeless at New Life would fight bitterly about which alley belonged to whom. They even fought over which mission bed they slept in, though all the cots were identical and cleaned daily. As best she could tell, it had something to do with vantage point, closeness to the door or to the bathroom, whatever. Bobman's viewpoint, his excuse, bless his heart, seemed to be a bit flawed.

Decisions, decided Liza, as she mopped up the serving table with paper towels. It's all about the decisions we make in life.

"So, about this woman…" Rosemary continued coming up behind Liza.

"What woman?" Kim said. The small, energetic woman had silently followed her partner into the serving area. "Beds are all made up and the laundry started," she told Rosemary, then waited expectantly, glancing back and forth between the other two. "There's a woman?"

Rosemary sighed and turned apologetic eyes toward her friend. "Liza met someone."

"No way! Who? Do I know her? I bet I do, I know everyone in this town." Her ice blue eyes lit with curiosity.

Liza had to laugh. Kim was a notorious busybody but a truly delightful person, so it took a while to realize she was masterfully pulling information from you. Kim had accompanied Rosemary home eight years ago from their time at a central Virginia college and they were still going strong. Liza couldn't think of a more perfectly matched couple. Kim was the flame to Rosemary's candle, and they complemented one another well.

"If only I'd had that with Gina," Liza murmured thoughtfully.

"Huh?" Kim wrinkled her nose and placed her hands on her slender hips. "Fess up, Liza honey. You can't keep a secret from us, you know. It never works."

"Believe me, I know. Truthfully, I don't know much about her. She bought the old Carson homestead over off Dooley."

"A guy bought that place," Rosemary said, drying her hands with a dishtowel. "Is she married?"

"No, of course not…I…" Liza frowned. She really didn't know. "How did you know it was a man?"

Rosemary shrugged. "I do read the newspaper, Liza honey. Even the property transactions. They're public records filed over there with Moses's bunch at the county courthouse."

"Ahh." Liza hadn't thought of that. "What was this owner's name?"

Her friend raised an eyebrow. "Please! You expect me to remember details like that?"

Kim giggled. "So, what's her name?"

"Shay. That's all I know." She went on to tell them in brief about the encounter at Dooley's Folly.

"So what made her so mad? What did you do?" Kim asked, chewing on a thumbnail. She rested one denim-clad hip on the side of the serving counter and crossed her feet in a nonchalant stance. She watched Liza with keen eyes. Her stare was unusual. It was odd to see such beautiful, cool blue eyes—natural ones—shining from such a dark Egyptian face. A shock of short spiky white-tipped dark hair above those eyes further added to the dichotomy.

"God knows. Some people are just born ornery," Liza answered.

Rosemary made a face at Kim. "Yep. That's the kind of person I'd be mooning about."

Liza growled playfully. "Just serve your damned sandwiches and hush."

Kim laughed and strolled away. Rosemary playfully pushed Liza before retreating to the kitchen for more sloppy joe filling.

CHAPTER EIGHT

Shay liked her new home. She had enjoyed the small home she'd owned in suburban Washington, DC, but hadn't been sorry to bid it farewell when the time had come. The home and grounds held far too many bad memories.

She knew she'd miss the large, custom-built dog compound out back as well as the convenience of being so close to a major city, but overall it hadn't been a bad trade.

She took another satisfying sip of hot coffee as she strolled across her back deck. She leaned forward and rested her forearms on the deck railing. Dappled sunlight frolicked along the edges of the yard as a calm breeze moved the trees.

Southern Alabama really was beautiful. Her parcel, the house and the acre lot surrounding it was, according to the realtors, a "prime historic venue." Somewhat hilly and surrounded by forest, the land soothed Shay, imparting a gentle peacefulness that she welcomed.

It had taken her several months to decide it was right for her, especially based on photos alone. After she'd clawed her way out of the deep emotional well she'd escaped into after Pepper's prosecution, she'd known the only path to full healing would be a move. Pepper's aura had permeated the DC home, souring it for Shay. She had cringed at the entry of every room, expecting an attack just inside every door. The closet, much like the one at Pepper's where she'd been locked for hour upon agonizing hour, seemed to mock her. And the sorrow she'd felt upon walking into the backyard, well, it was unbearable.

Now, as she stared out over the sparsely wooded land surrounding her 1960s ranch-style home, the idea of starting over and building something anew felt almost plausible. Her imagination envisioned a new and better compound, with covered runs and a long barn. She'd try that new Norwegian influence with family-style rooms instead of kennels. Cuddly sofas and old-fashioned Dutch doors seemed infinitely preferable to chain-link enclosures. She'd go radical and paint the outside lemon yellow to match her car.

She smiled and shook her head in disbelief. What was she thinking? Reluctantly, she turned to go back inside. She was still nervous about remaining exposed outside for too long.

Her eye caught the neighbor's house. From this vantage point, just outside the side door of her home, she could see the terra-cotta tile roof and upper veranda of the huge, mid-nineteenth century mansion. The elderly woman who lived there was out on the top deck again. Shay often saw her there in the mornings and, although nagged with guilt for her voyeuristic tendencies, would watch enraptured as the woman went through a series of yoga-style stretches. Pulling her gaze away was almost impossible due to the poetic beauty of the exercise. It was a stylistic welcome to the sun and Shay was touched each time she watched. Today the ritual was already over and the faceless rail-thin woman, white hair in a bun atop her head, was enjoying her own coffee, swaying back and forth in a tall rocking chair on the veranda.

Back inside, Shay double-locked the French doors, using a

burglar bar and a slide bolt. When she'd bought the house, she'd immediately had the steps leading from the ground to the deck outside removed, but the deck was only about five feet above ground level and still could be easily scaled.

Each time Shay entered her home, she felt a pang of loss because there was no dog to greet her. Since the age of twenty-seven, she'd had at least one dog—often more. Until this past three years. She sighed and moved to the bulletin board atop her makeshift desk.

There she was. Swampwitch Hattie Dawn von Deutscher. The photo had been taken at Lafayette Park in DC. It showed a much younger, happier Shay pressing cheek to cheek with the gorgeous fawn boxer. Hattie's flash had been minimal, so her color had been rich and extensive and almost the British red in tone. Shay had deliberately left her ears and tail uncropped, even knowing that meant she could never be a show dog. But that had been okay—she had been so much more to Shay. Hattie had been Shay's friend.

Tears welled in Shay's eyes and she turned from the photo. Heartbroken and feeling somewhat suicidal, she took huge gasping breaths, trying to employ techniques taught her by Dr. Frye. She rushed to the kitchen and placed both palms on the table for grounding. She leaned her body forward and closed her eyes. The counting began. With each number said aloud, she rocked backward while envisioning a good time with Hattie. One, Hattie as a puppy, newly birthed and clumsy. Two, Hattie patting Shay's leg with her puppy paws. Three, the adorable loopy grin. Four, one ear folded upon itself and tongue lolling from her mouth after rolling in the grass. Five, jogging along Pennsylvania Avenue, Hattie's stride erect and effortless. Six, training and Hattie's pout as she is reprimanded. Seven, Shay reading on the sofa, Hattie's head in her lap. Eight, velvet ears waiting to be rubbed. Nine, Hattie snoring gently in bed next to her. Ten, soft, hot kisses backed by not unpleasant doggie breath.

Breathing deeply, Shay forced away the other images. Of what she had discovered that October day, two years after escaping Pepper. She didn't remember the exact date, didn't want to. She knew it had been fall, after the first frost because of the layer of ice that had coated the cold, stiff...

A visceral cry escaped and Shay knew the horror hadn't gone. Might never go. There are things in this life that are unforgettable and finding Hattie that morning was one of them. Unforgettable and unforgivable. Finally realizing what a complete and utter monster Pepper was had enabled her to go after the woman with every bit of money and energy she could scrape together. What she had done to Shay had been secondary to what she had done to the dogs, to Hattie.

Shay's eyes roved madly around her home and lit on boxes still awaiting unpacking. She leapt toward them with a frantic burst of energy. Keeping busy wasn't a cure, but it would change the focus enough for her to survive.

CHAPTER NINE

Wicked Wings was rowdy. And it was only Friday night; Lord knew what Saturday would bring. Liza's brother Rich, cooking in the back, had only been out once for a perfunctory beer before hurrying back to flip burgers and sop wings in barbecue sauce. A huge platter of said wings rested in front of Liza and they were disappearing fast. Luckily, wings weren't a particular favorite of hers, but she did enjoy seeing the joy Arlie Russell experienced from munching them.

Arlie *was* enjoying them. Liza had to smile at the large woman's enthusiasm. Without pause in her intense conversation with Rosemary, Arlie palmed a handful of wings and dropped them onto her plate. She swiped her sauce-covered hand on one of a pile of soiled napkins next to her unused fork and took a mighty swig of beer. Rosemary snagged a wing off Arlie's plate and nibbled it as she nodded agreement with something Arlie said. Arlie caught Liza's fond gaze and smiled at her, a gold tooth gleaming in the bright glow from one of the many televisions lining the walls.

"Hey, Liza. You eating or what?"

"Of course, if you leave me some."

"Ass. There's more in the back. You don't have to worry."

Liza laughed and gently kicked Arlie's leg under the table. "Just giving you a hard time, Woodpecker."

"How is everything over at the lumberyard?" Kim asked. "We haven't heard you talk about it much lately."

Kim seemed a little tired today, not her usual vivacious, annoying self. Even her short, spiky hair seemed flat.

Arlie mopped at her mouth. "Too much work. I don't have time even to talk about it. There's tons of houses going up east of town. We're doing all the lumber for that, even some of the prefab."

"Wow. That's the new subdivision. What's it called?" Kim leaned forward and cupped her chin in one propped up hand.

"Whispering Pines," interjected Mindy Quintero, placing her tray on Arlie's lap. She rested her hands on Arlie's shoulders. Arlie, in a tender gesture, laid her cheek against one of them in a brief caress. "As if pine really whispers. Those names are sometimes so stupid."

"Hey, pines whisper like crazy when the wind blows. You just have to be quiet and listen," Liza responded.

"No one's quiet anymore," commented Kim, looking around the noisy restaurant as if for emphasis. "That's what's wrong with the whole country."

Liza caught Rosemary's eye. Ro shrugged meaningfully, as if letting Liza know she had no idea why her partner was in such poor spirits.

"I know, Kim," Mindy commiserated. "I'm not so sure I like the way our world's turning out. I wish we could have a life like our parents."

"I don't know about that," Arlie said. "A big bad dyke like me would have had a harder time then than I do now."

Mindy pressed her lips to Arlie's cheek, her hands smoothing

Arlie's closely shorn hair. "I know, baby. I'm glad things are easier for you now that everyone's a little more accepting."

"Only a precious little," interjected Kim, sourly.

"Hey, who peed in your Cheerios?" asked Mindy, leaning back and putting her hands on her hips. "No negativity allowed."

Kim was taken aback, as if she hadn't realized the extent of her bad mood. She laughed suddenly, momentarily transforming into her usual bubbly self. "I'm sorry, guys. I'm just letting the stories get to me, rape, abuse. Sometimes it really does bother me, you know?"

"Must have been a rough day at the mission," Liza said.

"We've got this new couple in. The woman is just out of a really bad relationship, abusive. She was beaten, raped and cheated on by this alcoholic demon," Kim continued soberly.

"It's horrible," agreed Rosemary. "I feel so bad for her." She nodded toward Liza, "It's that new one you met yesterday."

"But look who she's with now—another drunk. And she's traveling all over the country with him. What is she thinking?" Kim's voice was low, almost a hiss of contempt.

"She's not thinking...at all," said Liza calmly. She could tell Kim was really worked up about the situation. "I'll never understand why women feel like they deserve to be mistreated. And why, when they're offered the opportunity to leave, they don't. It makes no sense to me." She paused. "But then, I'm not in their shoes."

Kim sighed. "I don't know why I do this, sometimes. Seems just as stupid."

"It's all the glamour and the big paychecks," Rosemary offered.

The women laughed as one, but the laughter had an edge. All had been touched by homelessness. It seemed like a futile issue, but they knew the fight to remedy the situation would continue.

"Think of the ones you help," said Patty Huffner as she pulled out an empty chair and joined them. "Before you guys came along and got Doc to see them, I used to have homeless people in my office every week looking for pain meds or antibiotics. And I'm a vet, for Chrissakes! Y'all do good work and don't forget it."

"Here! Here!" Liza agreed, raising her mug of beer in a toast. "Let's hear it for New Life!"

"To New Life Mission," the women chorused as one, lifting their glasses.

Liza spied her then, a small ethereal woman with red hair who was entering the dimly lit restaurant. It was a familiar face, one that had been haunting her. Liza knew her right away.

"No way," Liza whispered while realizing that, of course their paths would cross again, both living in the same small town.

Arlie, who many thought oblivious to the subtleties around her, was actually quite observant.

"What is it?" she asked, leaning toward Liza. Her words alerted Mindy, who also leaned close. Soon Rosemary, Kim and Patty quieted and turned to Liza. The entire group of women turned as one to follow Liza's intense gaze.

"Who is she?" asked Kim.

Rosemary shook her head as if awakening from a dream. She emitted a low whistle of appreciation. "Is that her?" She looked at Liza.

"Who? Is that who?" Arlie stared from woman to woman.

"Liza's new friend," Rosemary answered absently.

"Ro!" Liza whispered, her tone irritated. "She's a woman I met the other day," she explained. "Her name is Shay."

"Well, go get her. Let's meet this Shay," Arlie said, grinning. Liza shot her a warning glance but rose and made her way across the crowded room.

A relieved expression settled on Shay's face when she saw Liza approaching. She looked as though she'd been ready to leave the loud, unwelcoming environment.

"Hello," Liza said loudly. The din in the bar part of the restaurant was deafening. "Shay, right?"

"Right. Yes. And listen, I'm really sorry about the other day. I have one of those Irish tempers that goes off without warning."

Liza was having a hard time hearing Shay but recognized the apology. "No problem. That's all done." She leaned close. "I'm Liza, by the way. Come on over and sit with us." She indicated the table where her friends watched with avid curiosity.

Liza studied Shay, watching as doubt and fear kaleidoscoped

on her lovely face. Finally, courage won out and she nodded. Liza took the smaller hand in hers and led her through the maze of haphazardly placed tables and chairs filled with boisterous drinkers.

Once they were in the quieter restaurant area, Liza sighed. "That's better." She smiled encouragement at Shay as she spoke to the others. "Hey, guys, this is Shay."

Shay examined each face briefly and nodded a shy hello.

Arlie stood, almost dropping Mindy's serving tray, and extended her right hand. Realizing that it was spattered with wing sauce, she withdrew it, scrubbed it against her denim overshirt, and then offered it again. Liza laughed and rolled her eyes for Ro's amusement.

"I'm Arlie, Arlie Russell, and this is my wife, Mindy."

Mindy, who had expertly caught the tray falling from Arlie's lap, nudged Arlie aside.

"Hi there," she said, extending her hand. "Nice to meet you, Shay. Can I get you a beer to start?"

"Mich would be good, if you have it," Shay responded.

"Be right back." Mindy hurried off.

"Rosemary King," Rosemary said, rising to shake Shay's hand.

Kim, studying Shay with keen eyes, stood and offered her hand. "And I'm Kim, Ro's better half. This is Patty, our local vet. Here, sit, join us." She indicated the chair Liza had purloined from a nearby table.

Returning Patty's welcoming nod, Shay took a seat next to Liza.

"So, Shay, where are you from?" Rosemary asked. "What brought you to our quaint little burg?"

Shay grimaced as if reliving an unpleasant memory. "My parents passed away, so there was no reason to stay in Virginia. This seemed like a quiet, nice place to live." She shrugged and her gaze wandered the crowded restaurant. "So here I am."

"Do you have kids?" Kim queried. Her curiosity had been piqued by Shay's easy acceptance of their introductions as partners.

"No, no kids. And no husband." Her pale lips compressed into a thin line as if expecting a challenge.

Mindy approached with a bottle and a frosted mug. "Here's your beer, hon."

Liza cringed, remembering the time she had called Shay "hon."

"Thanks, Mindy. Just the bottle's okay." Shay did not explode as Liza expected, merely plucked the bottle off the tray, leaving the mug behind.

Mindy hurried off, to check on her other tables.

"You're living in the old Carson homestead up off Dooley, aren't you?" said Liza.

Shay nodded. "Yes, by that weird pond."

Liza smiled cautiously. "Right. Dooley's Folly."

Arlie spoke up around a mouthful of french fries. "So, how'd y'all meet anyway?"

Shay laughed and blushed, her fair skin glowing crimson in the TV lights. She politely gestured for Liza to tell the story. Liza related the entire incident, excluding the extent of Shay's temper. In the tale, Liza made herself more of a villain angering the fair maiden until the maiden stormed off. Back to her castle.

"That's hilarious," Rosemary said, even though she'd heard part of the story before. "Stuck in Dooley's Folly. Too funny."

"It wasn't funny at the time, that's for sure," Shay added, sipping her cold beer.

CHAPTER TEN

"Wow, fresh air," Liza said, inhaling deeply as they stepped outside Wicked Wings. "I don't know why CM lets people smoke in the main dining room. It's bad enough in the bar."

"It's the whole bar-type atmosphere," suggested Shay. "I think people actually enjoy the illicit thrill. He'd have less business otherwise."

Though enjoying the company of Liza's friends, Shay had been glad when Liza suggested a walking tour of downtown Maypearl. The sultry night air was oddly refreshing. Crickets and other night insects serenaded them from the surrounding forest as they walked along.

"You could be right," Liza agreed.

They took a right and walked north along Esperanza toward a buff-colored strip mall. A large sign proclaimed it Sunset Mall, but it had never lived up to this grandiose name, consisting of merely a half-dozen ordinary glass-fronted businesses set into tan stucco and decorative brick.

"This belongs to Surep Dujan," Liza said pausing at the large window of a small Subway restaurant. Dim night-lights lit the empty interior and signs filled with piles of moisture-kissed vegetables beckoned to them irresistibly. "I'm sure he's home with his beautiful wife, Duri, and their two well-behaved sons. He's very much a family man."

Shay nodded. "A good thing," she murmured.

"Have you met Doctor King yet? He's our local sawbones."

"No, I haven't been sick, thank goodness. Why?" Shay responded.

"His wife, Paula, runs this place." They paused before a huge plate glass window decorated with a red rose logo and the banner *Paula's Posies*. "He's Ro's brother, too, in case no one told you."

"Original," Shay commented pointing toward the logo.

"You'd have to meet her," Liza said, grinning.

Shay paused at the next storefront. Styrofoam heads peered blankly from shelves like blind ghosts trapped behind the eerie plate glass. Each head wore a differently styled wig, some with garish colors.

"Oh my," Shay exclaimed. "Atomic Hair Designs?"

Liza laughed and shoved her hands deep into the pockets of her jeans. "That's Lisa Adams. She was the one all the boys chased after in high school. Larry Adams won out. Shame, too, because, between you and me, she could have done a lot better."

Shay nodded and they moved on toward the colonial façade of Mac Wayne's Allstate Insurance office. An 8 x 10 glossy photo of Mac's plump, freckled face crowned by a patch of red hair smiled out at them. Shay walked faster as Liza chuckled.

"Mmm, smell that?" Liza asked a moment later.

"What is it?" Shay lifted her nose and inhaled deeply.

"Coffee. I swear Nora puts roasted coffee beans in the Java Cup's air vents to draw us suckers in."

"Even at night?"

"Oh, yeah, she's devious."

They laughed companionably.

"So, this is it," Liza sighed.

Shay looked around in disbelief. "What? You're not serious?"

"Yeah, I am. I mean, this is the heart of Maypearl. There's a couple businesses out your way and a couple back that way, toward where I live. Oh, and if you bear right off Esperanza, heading north, you'll come to the dollar store and the car parts place."

She paused and gestured toward the street. "The post office and library are over there and all the schools are east of town, off Esperanza, and that's pretty much it. Surely you checked it out?"

Shay was embarrassed and felt a little defensive. "Well, I've been busy, settling in. I've only been here about a week."

"You didn't check out the town before you bought the Carson place?"

"No," Shay said, exasperation showing. "I didn't. I had someone else do it."

Ah, that explained the man her grandmother had spoken with. Liza stayed silent for a long beat. "So, why did you move here, Shay? There has to be a reason. It wasn't for Maypearl's deep Southern charm, obviously."

They turned and walked back the way they'd come. The question hung between them and Liza could see Shay struggling with how much she would say to Liza. Though tempted to reassure her, Liza knew this was Shay's battle.

"I just wanted to get away," she said finally. "I needed to."

A mantle of intimacy had fallen over the two of them with the admission. Liza took a deep breath of anticipation, inhaling Shay's unique coconut scent. The intimacy felt good.

"Do you want to talk about it? About what happened? Was it a bad breakup?"

"Yes, sort of. The details aren't important. I simply needed to be safe. Alabama seemed a good long way from DC. I…I once had family here." She shrugged. "It just seemed to fit somehow. I like the South."

Liza looked at Shay and in the sudden light outside Wicked Wings, their eyes met. The gazes coupled and held for a handful of heartbeats.

"I'm glad," Liza said simply. The words seemed automatic

because she was held spellbound in the tractor beam of Shay's cobalt eyes. Liza saw so much there—a curious nature, the fire of conviction, a fear as yet unnamed. A connection was forged, and suddenly afraid and confused, Liza pulled her gaze away.

"Here we are," she added, as if emerging from a dream. "Back at Wings."

"Your brother is nice. I like him," Shay interjected. "How long has he worked here?"

"Forever. Since high school."

"He must like it then."

Liza smiled and shook her head. "CM spoils him, is all. Richie hasn't worked a hard lick, ever." She sobered. "He took Mama's death hard. He was her baby boy."

"I'm sorry your mama passed," Shay said quietly. She studied her entwining fingers as if she'd never seen them before. For some strange reason, maybe loneliness, she seemed loath to leave Liza's company.

"It was her heart," Liza said with a shrug of helplessness. "Runs in her family."

"Still."

"I know."

"Both my parents are gone now. They were older." Shay turned to study Liza. "Can you imagine what a shock I was? They thought they couldn't have children, then, in their fifties, here I come."

Liza laughed aloud, as if imagining the disbelief Shay's parents must have experienced.

"Not that they weren't happy about it," Shay continued, "just…well, it's late to start a family. I felt a little like an afterthought, like a third wheel, because they had developed such a great relationship. Their love was so powerful that after Mother died from pneumonia Papa just pined away for her. He didn't last three months, joining her in his sleep one night."

"I like the idea that they might be back together," Liza commented softly.

"Me too," Shay responded, smiling sadly.

"You coming back in?" Liza indicated the restaurant.

Indecision battled within Shay.

"No. I don't think so." She looked around nervously, afraid of the sudden and powerful feelings she had for Liza. This certainly was not part of her master plan. She enjoyed Liza's quiet gentleness, however, which was so very different from Pepper's hyper angst. It felt good. Too good. It terrified her on so many levels, levels she didn't want to address tonight. "I'll go home."

Liza examined Shay for several silent minutes. Shay chafed under the placid scrutiny. "Okay," she agreed finally. "Let me walk you to your car?"

"It's just over here. I'll be fine." Shay hated the distrustful thoughts that filled her. She was torn between seeking Liza's protection and the worry that Liza wanted to walk her to the car so she could track her later, maybe follow her home. Pepper had done it so easily once when Shay had moved to escape her.

"I'll watch until you get there, all right?"

"All right." Turning away abruptly, Shay clasped one hand to her mouth, hating that she thought the way she did. Years of caution had fed her newly suspicious nature.

"Hey, Shay, do you like dogs?"

Liza's low voice arrested her and her heart pounded with new fear. What did Liza know? She lowered the hand and turned slowly. "Yes. Why?"

"Do you know where the animal shelter is? Over on Professional Drive?"

"No. I don't even know where Professional is."

Liza laughed. "Guess not, since you know absolutely nothing about Maypearl. You know Esperanza, right?"

At Shay's cautious nod, she continued, pointing north.

"You just take a right off Esperanza onto Preserve Trail. Go about a mile and take another right on Professional. I'll be at the shelter tomorrow about ten to help out and walk the dogs. Come over if you can. We always have a good time."

Shay studied Liza's sweet face, with its corona of unruly blond hair. "I might do that, Liza."

Liza nodded and smiled as she leaned one shoulder against the side of the wood-shingled building. She made it evident she would wait there until Shay made it safely to her car.

CHAPTER ELEVEN

"He's just so bad-tempered…I guess the tumors must hurt him," Christine said sadly. She was securely holding a bedraggled hunk of Himalayan cat. The animal was clearly uncomfortable. He was eying Liza as if she could serve as his blood-filled breakfast.

"I can see that. So is Patty going to put him down?"

"I'm afraid so." Christine sighed. "There's no way we could place him. Any family that took him would be shredded in no time."

"He'd probably run away too, be back on the streets. Shame, though." Liza carefully reached out. The cat squalled an angry warning. She drew the hand away.

Christine loosened her paralyzing grip on the wriggling cat's neck and returned him to his cage.

Animals didn't seem to be close to Christine's heart, but Liza could tell she was a hard worker and that counted for a lot. Paul had called Ro yesterday with a progress report on the first two days and he was happy with her energy, her initiative and her attendance. Liza felt a great sense of relief upon hearing this. The New Life gals had been burned before when recommending homeless people for local work.

"So how's the job working out here?"

"I like it," Christine replied, wiping her gloved hands on a paper towel. "Rosemary sure has this town in hand, doesn't she?"

"She sure does," Liza said, laughing. "She knows everyone and is great at networking. Better than me, that's for sure. Must be from all that time in college."

They walked toward the dog kennels, and Liza bent to scratch Maizie's ears. Maizie, a beautiful Sheltie mix, had quickly become a shelter favorite. The dog leaned her head closer to the cage wall to ensure that Liza's fingers could reach as much ear as possible. The surrounding dogs set up a chorus that was deafening.

"You're no slouch either from what I hear. Is it true you provide food for all them dogs?"

Liza stood and Maizie's tail wagged her body as she waited for Liza to resume the attention or open her cage. Liza smiled at her eagerness. "Later, Maizie girl. We'll be back."

"Not exactly," she responded loudly to Chris's comment as they moved along the noisy row of kennels. "Our company, Meadows Produce, provides vegetables to this mill near Greenville. They use the carrots and squash and whatnot to mix with the meat products. Part of the meal is then sent here for Carol and Paul to use for feed. We also barter produce for the trucking so there's no cost there."

They stepped through into a hall leading to the quieter office area.

"What does the mill charge for the feed?" Christine asked as they entered the office.

Paul Critchfield, the tall, thin shelter director, answered without lifting his balding head from the account books. "She won't tell. It's their donation and she won't even let us know how much they give. Weird."

"I think it's kind of cool. Like a big charity mystery," interjected Carol, his wife.

Liza paused just inside the open office door, listening as the frantic barking died down to indignant chuffs in the kennel area. She studied Paul and Carol. She'd known them since she was a kid. They never seemed to age. Carol was big into yoga and Liza surmised that in it she'd found a fountain of youth. Paul was simply one of those old hippies who only improve with age. They'd been running the animal shelter for as long as Liza could remember and did it very well. Active in soliciting local support, the Critchfields and the shelter were icons, a prime example of excellent management.

"Well, thanks for that, Carol. Truth is, our fields produce so well, if we didn't donate, some of it would go to waste. It's a win-win for both sides."

"I knew the little animals did, but I didn't know dogs and cats eat vegetables," Christine said, shaking her head. Her dark salt-and-pepper hair had been pulled back into a ponytail. Liza noticed a curved scar that ran along her hairline, a scar usually hidden when her hair was down.

Liza realized at the same time that she had finally become accustomed to Christine's missing teeth and no longer even noticed the lack.

"They do, dogs especially. It's healthier when there's a good ratio of veggies to meat. It gives them a lot of the nutrients they need," Liza responded.

"If I had my way about it," grunted Paul, turning away from his books and facing them. "I'd have a vegetarian shelter."

"Why can't you?" Christine looked surprised.

"Some shelter owners do, I bet. The local SPCA group funds us, though, and their vet recommends a mix," he added. "Dogs and cats are carnivorous, they say, but I have friends who feed vegetables only. Their pets are fine."

"Well, at least using Green Pride's feed we get some veggies into them," Liza offered.

Carol rose from her desk and stretched gracefully. "Okay, Chris. It's time to let the dogs out for their run so we can clean the kennels. Are you ready?"

Christine nodded and moved toward the door.

"Oh, Carol," Liza said. "I invited someone to come by and help with the socialization. Her name is Shay, and she claims to like the little beasties. I know you're always short on volunteers so maybe she'll become a regular."

"That would be great," Carol said as she entered the main hallway releasing a torrent of expectant dog sound just outside. "Do we have any paid positions, Paul?"

Paul shook his head in the negative. "Nope. Chris got the last one. April's moving in February so you can have her check back then."

Liza laughed cheerfully. "You guys are something else. I hadn't thought about a job for her. I don't even know what she does, or if she's currently working. I'll let her know, though."

Paul nodded. "Good. We don't have that slot filled yet so tell her soon."

"You mean Ro hasn't sent someone over yet?" Sarcasm dripped from her voice.

"Not yet," Paul said as he moved to follow his wife.

"Can you do cat care today, Liza?" Carol called back to her.

Liza nodded and waved her on.

Half an hour later, Liza was pleasantly surprised to see Shay drive up. Liza watched as she got out of the car and walked around, studying the shelter buildings. Seeing Shay made her feel warm in the heart region, but she didn't take the time to ponder it now. She closed Caspurr's cage with a whispered apology and headed through the office.

"Well, hello. You made it!" Liza welcomed Shay as she entered through the double-paned glass door. She wanted to hug her but refrained. "Welcome to the Maypearl Animal Shelter."

"It's so nice," commented Shay as she looked around. "I especially like the way it's laid out so you can see the kennels as you drive up."

"It's a cool design. Al Jonas, over at the sawmill, got his sons together and they did it all in their spare time. He said he wanted people to see the animals right away...so they'd adopt them."

"That makes sense. Has it been working?"

Liza shrugged. "We seem to do okay. More get taken home than put down. Always a good thing."

Shay twisted her hands together nervously. "So, how can I help? You said something about walking dogs?"

"Yep, but it's mostly just companionship. You pet them and give them atta girls and atta boys when they fetch and carry. Stuff like that."

"Hmm, my favorite activities," Shay replied.

"Well, Chris and Carol are already running the dogs while they clean so we have cat duty first. That way the dogs'll be calmer when we get to them. You like cats, right?"

"Absolutely. We always had them when I was growing up."

Liza tilted her head and smiled at Shay. "Good. Come with me."

Shay followed Liza into the cat area and immediately began cooing to the responsive cats. Even the pain-wracked Himalayan almost warmed to the redhead.

"I'm working on Caspurr's kennel over here. There's only one more. Can you do the kittens on the end there?"

"Sure. I just love the little guys," Shay replied, her voice eager. "What do you want me to do exactly?"

"Just feed and water and replace the litter. You can use this cleaner on the litter pan. Then you kind of look the cats over and make sure they have clean bottoms and eyes."

Liza tucked the lovable Caspurr into her left elbow and used the other hand to scoop fresh food into the cat's dish.

A small series of pained exclamations startled her, and she whirled to see that one of the kittens had decided to practice mountain climbing on Shay's shoulder and scalp.

"Ow! That hurts, you little monster." Shay struggled to remove the mountain climber while simultaneously closing the cage so his three kitty siblings wouldn't escape. The red tabby settled on Shay's head like a Sunday-go-to-meeting hat, his brown and yellow striped tail dangling between Shay's eyes. The kitten's back legs scrambled for purchase on either side of Shay's head, disarranging her long hair and shoving it into her face. Shay's hand stayed its upward ascent, and she stood still as if disbelieving her predicament.

Liza's laugh bubbled up from deep within and although she fought to squelch it, it escaped nevertheless.

Shay turned her cat-adorned head and looked at Liza, eliciting further laughter. Her face morphed back and forth between anger, embarrassment and laughter. Luckily, laughter won out this time, and she reached up to carefully remove the kitten and place him back into the cage.

"I'm gonna call you Brown Sugar," she crooned to the cat. "Cause you're just so sweet." Her voice dripped sarcastic saccharine. She pushed the disheveled hair back behind her ears and dabbed her fingers at her head searching for blood.

"The Claw is more like it," Liza offered, returning Caspurr to her freshened kennel and hurrying to help Shay handle the fast-moving bundles of fur.

"So," Liza sighed, watching Shay as they washed their hands later at the utility sink. "Are you ready for the dogs?"

"Bring them on," Shay said, laughing. "Let's hope they don't have spiny little needle claws." She squeezed the soap and it slipped from her hands and flew high. Liza leaned and caught it before it hit the floor.

Liza grinned as Shay blushed. She would never forget the sight of Shay wearing the kitten hat. "As accident prone as you seem to be, you should be glad we're not working with any that bite."

CHAPTER TWELVE

By the time the two made their way outside with the dogs, the sun had mercifully moved lower in the sky. A cool breeze had found its way into the Gulf as well and had come inland. It teased at the sweat on Liza's brow, and she pulled at the front of her T-shirt, tenting it as if to invite the wind inside.

"It sure is a beautiful day," Shay commented as they entered the fenced-in dog paddock.

Liza breathed deeply, "It is that."

Although the two dozen or so dogs had been clustered around Carol at the far end, they quickly abandoned her and bounded over to Liza and Shay as soon as the gate slapped shut.

Shay, the smaller of the two, almost lost her footing in the ensuing melee, but Liza steadied her as she reprimanded the animals. Shay took the onslaught in stride, however, and was soon on her knees with an arm slung around two of the dogs while others licked every inch of her face.

"Well, it's a cinch she likes dogs," Carol commented as she approached.

Hearing her, Shay stood and extended her hand even as the wagging tails of her new friends pummeled her sideways.

"Hi, I'm Shay Raynor," she said introducing herself to Carol before Liza had a chance.

"Carol. It's nice to meet you, Shay. Thank you for coming out to help with the dogs."

"I've always loved dogs. My mom handled Corgis so I never needed an alarm clock when I was growing up. I usually had a dog licking me awake."

Carol laughed as she fondled an Irish setter's ears. "Story of my life. We always have a houseful. How many do you have now?"

Liza, her senses strangely attuned to Shay, picked up the subtle pause before answered. "None. Too much moving around, I guess."

"Well, when you get settled, we have lots to choose from, as you can see."

Shay laughed and knelt to hug a retriever mix they called Bundy. "I'll keep that in mind."

"Look at you!" Carol cried explosively. Shay and Liza looked up in surprise, soon realizing Carol was talking to one of the dogs. "You've rubbed a bare spot on your ear." She was chiding a young Jack Russell terrier. "Now we've got to go treat it."

She scooped the dog into her arms and hurried away. "I'll see you ladies later. Let me know if you need anything!"

"Whirlwind," Shay commented dryly.

"Yes," Liza agreed with a sigh.

Shay cooed to her circle of dogs, scratching behind every ear presented while Liza led a second gang a short distance away for a game of fetch. Hours passed as the two worked the dogs. Eventually the entire group reclined on the grassy expanse, sweating and panting, pleasantly exhausted.

"Well, that was fun," Shay said, holding her heavy hair off her neck. "It sure gets hot here in crazy Alabama."

Liza smiled, surprised that Shay recalled their conversation at Dooley's.

"Yep. I like the heat, though. There's something so much more alive here than in colder places."

Shay leaned back and rested her weight on bent elbows. "How do you mean?"

"Things don't die out. Bugs, plants. You know. I like that. Plants grow all year in the South."

Shay swatted at a fly and laughed. "Yeah, and we mustn't forget the bugs."

Liza joined in the merriment. The sound caused one of the dogs to rise and meander over to lick at Liza's nose.

"C'mon, Scarlet. It's too hot to be carryin' on that way." Liza nevertheless scratched the dog between the ears. Scarlet closed her eyes and leaned into Liza's hand. "I think border collies are some of the friendliest dogs, don't you?"

Shay squinted at Liza. "Yeah, I do. But you know she's an Aussie cattle dog, right?"

"No way," Liza replied immediately. "She's a border mix."

Shay sat up and scrubbed dried grass off her arms. "No, seriously Liza, I know. She's a cattle girl."

"I disagree. Look at the markings. If she were a cattle dog, she'd have less of a blaze, not the linear markings like Scarlet has. They're border collie markings. I know the size is the same and they're close, but I really think this is border."

Shay eyed Liza evenly. "How familiar are you with Australian cattle dogs? I know an awful lot about them. Have you even looked at her muzzle, her ears? This is definitely a cattle dog mix."

Liza studied Scarlet and then shook her head, eyes closed. "You're wrong. What would a cattle dog be doing in southern Alabama anyway?"

Shay bristled and clamped her small teeth together as if to help forestall losing her temper. "Liza, this is *not* a border collie, and I'd really appreciate it if you'd let it go. I know what I'm talking about."

"Shay, I'm not doubting your knowledge. I just know you're dead wrong on this one." Liza was trying to be reasonable. She remembered keenly Shay's Irish temper.

Shay was getting angrier by the minute and her voice had risen. "*How* do you know? Who told you? I should say, what *idiot* told you this was a border collie?"

Scarlet, not understanding the altercation, stared from woman to woman, moving back in alarm as Liza leapt to her feet, followed quickly by Shay.

"What do you mean, idiot? I checked this dog in myself. I've been doing it for years and was taught to identify the dogs by Paul, Carol's husband. He runs the shelter and knows more about dogs than the two of us put together."

Shay had crossed her arms across her chest and was watching Liza with a challenging stare. "Oh, really. So maybe Paul's the one I need to talk to, not his apprentice dog whisperer."

There was a definite sneer in her voice, and Liza's eyes widened in indignation. "What the hell do you mean by that?!"

"Just what I said." Shay lowered her arms, her hands balled into fists at her sides. She appeared ready for anything Liza might say to her.

"Ladies? Is there a problem?" Carol had approached the paddock as the two women argued. She studied their angry faces. "I don't think you're setting a very good example for the dogs, do you?"

Liza couldn't help smiling as she backed down. "No, we're not."

Shay's cheeks were pink from a day of sun and her waning anger. Liza thought she looked adorable.

"What do you think, Carol? Is Scarlet a border collie?" Liza pulled her eyes from Shay.

Carol studied Scarlet, who was trying to engage Maizie in some leaping dog play. "No, I think she's a cattle dog. One of the Australian ones. They come from dingos, you know..." Carol broke off as Shay let loose a yelp of victory.

"I *told* you. I *told* you she was!" Shay punched her fist into the sky and whirled about in a dance of triumph.

Liza's mouth fell open and a deep flush moved from her neck along her cheekbones. She closed her mouth abruptly and cleared her throat, determined to learn from the embarrassment. She ignored Shay and turned to Carol. "How can you tell for sure?"

Carol, eyebrows lifted in surprise, pulled her gaze from Shay and motioned for Scarlet to come to them. "Touch her back."

Liza leaned and pressed both palms along the dog's broad back. "So?"

"Dig your fingers into the fur? There. Feel that undercoat... it's kind of oily? Borders have much finer fur. There's longer fur on a border but it's finer in texture. That's really the only way to tell, especially when there's Border somewhere back in the line."

Liza glanced sideways at Shay, who had quieted and was now listening to the other two. "So, there is border in there? Why are you saying she's more ACD than border?"

Carol's hand lay along Scarlet's back in an absent-minded caress. "A lot of the cattle dogs have border in them now. As a match, it's a good one."

"Look at the markings," Liza interrupted. "They look more like..."

"Look at the hindquarters though," Carol said insistently. "See the brindling? That's a cattle dog trait. As are the brown eyebrows. Borders just have the mask."

As if understanding Carol, Scarlet turned her cute face toward Liza, showing off the deep tan of her eyebrows. Her tongue lolled from her mouth. It looked as though she were grinning at Liza.

"Don't feel bad, Liza," Shay added. "It's an honest mistake. Scarlet does have an exceptionally dark mask and other markings. I wouldn't have known if not for her rough coat and the brindling."

Liza appreciated Shay's attempt to make her feel better, but the embarrassment lingered. "Ah well, it's good to learn something new every day."

Carol smiled. "True. Hey, have either of you seen Chris? I wanted her to help round up the dogs, but she's wandered off."

Liza's eyes roamed the shelter grounds. "I don't see her. We'll help you, though. Have you got the leads?"

"I'll get them. You two start getting the littler ones together and we'll take them first."

CHAPTER THIRTEEN

"This isn't your car," Liza said accusingly. "Is it? This wasn't the one you had last night."

Shay laughed. "I didn't think you'd notice. That one was a loaner," she explained. "This relic was in being babied and soothed into another ten thousand miles."

She patted the hood of the classic '77 Beetle. It was vintage but painted a bright lemon yellow.

Liza looked at Shay as if she'd grown a pair of wings. "I would have remembered this car."

Shay smiled proudly.

Liza smoothed her hand across the baby-bottom decklid. "Wait a minute. I don't know much about cars, really, but I know you can't find these parts anymore. This looks like it must have when coming off the showroom floor."

She peered inside. "Even the vinyl bucket seats! And the original over-sized steering wheel."

She straightened her back and squinted at Shay. "Okay, now

I know. You're rich, right? How much work have you had done to this?" She turned away but whirled to face Shay again. "No, don't tell me. It looks new. Is it the original air-cooled engine?"

Shay had endeavored to speak several times, each time cut off when Liza blasted her with a new question. Finally she spoke, her voice calm and slow in an effort to counteract Liza's excitement. "I have a collector friend. He's helped me get parts. I actually bought it from him after he'd done most of the work. I had a hard time getting him to part with it."

"I bet it cost you a mint," Liza said. She rested her head and right arm on the hood while her left hand caressed the nose.

Shay shrugged. "I had a good job at the time. It's paid for so all I have is the upkeep. And my friend Thomas, who lives in South Carolina now, said that if I didn't keep it in top condition, he'd come find me and take it back home with him. Which, I know, he still believes is where it belongs."

"I hear they're hard to maintain?"

Shay laughed. "Well, you should have seen the mechanic's face when I drove in."

"Where did you take it?"

"I had to go into Mobile. It's the only VW dealership around." She paused and tilted her head to one side. "He actually reacted kind of like you just reacted. That and very, very happy."

"Why?" Liza pressed the nose handle, amazed that the release button still worked.

"Maintenance, I guess. He knows how often I'll be in for oil changes and valve adjustments. He even drove it back from Mobile this morning, just so he could have a road trip in it."

Liza realized suddenly that Shay had a cute little dimple in her left cheek. It wasn't deep or even that noticeable. Just, there was a certain way she smiled and it would appear. Held spellbound by this realization, Liza stood her ground as Shay approached the nose.

"I hope you don't mind, but I packed a lunch for us. I hope things are still cool. It's gotten late." Shay's hands gently brushed Liza's aside as she released the hood and lifted out a large wicker basket.

Brought back to her senses by the mention of food, Liza was

thrilled and her face mirrored that joy. "Mind? Not hardly. I'm starving. Whatcha got in there?" She eyed the basket, and her sturdy, square hands fluttered toward it in anticipation.

Shay watched Liza, her gaze dancing merrily. "It's easy to see the way to your heart…food!"

Embarrassed anew, Liza looked away. "I do like to eat," she admitted. "But it's not the only way to my heart." She turned back, fixing Shay in a smoldering gaze.

Shay, as she had the night before, stood transfixed by the power of Liza's raw sensual energy. Liza's eyes were so warm and inviting that, when stoked with passionate feeling, they were downright mesmerizing.

Tearing her gaze away, Shay coughed nervously. "Well, where shall we eat?"

"Lemme see," Liza continued, reaching toward the basket.

"My, you're persistent." She opened the lid and peered inside. "Let's see…there's wine, a Riesling, my personal favorite. I hope you like it. Also sandwiches. You didn't seem overly enamored with the chicken wings last night, so I went with a nice Gouda and some tomatoes, sweet onions and lettuce. Hope you like mustard. Then there's fruit for dessert, grapes and some local citrus."

Shay looked up and was taken aback by the tender look on Liza's face. Before she knew what was happening, Liza had enveloped her in a warm, close hug. The subtle waft of Liza's sandalwood scent made Shay's knees weaken.

"Where have you been all my life?" Liza whispered close to her ear. The sound of Liza's whisper and the sensation of Liza's warm breath on her neck made Shay's knees give way completely, and she collapsed into Liza's arms.

"Whoa now," Liza said gently, holding Shay closer. "Are you okay?"

Crimson from head to toe, Shay pulled away and studied Liza as if the other woman had threatened her life. Shay knew she should run as far and as fast as possible. She *knew* this but…she so very wanted to stay. Even though Liza's closeness made her feel as though her whole world was spinning, there was still this element of safety with her. Shay felt protected, more so than ever before, especially since Pepper had entered her life. Her decision was made in a split second. She couldn't run forever. She turned away and pulled a small round tablecloth from the nose.

"I'm fine, Liza. You just caught me off guard. I'm glad you like the lunch." She hugged the tablecloth close. "Where shall we eat?"

Liza seemed pleased by Shay's ridiculous reaction. "Come with me," she said lightly, taking the laden basket from her.

Shay followed Liza and, when Liza held the door open for her, hesitated only briefly before climbing into the passenger seat of Liza's white Tacoma pickup. She caressed the soft gray cloth of the bench seat as Liza paused to stow the basket in the truck bed.

"Wow, what a truck," she commented as Liza slid into the driver's side.

"Well," drawled Liza pointedly, "it's not a lemon yellow Volkswagen, but it'll have to do."

Shay smiled, glad she had decided to deal with the extreme feeling the taller woman engendered in her. She resolved to forget about the feelings for now and examine them later when she was alone and safe from Liza's knowing gaze.

"Where are we going?" she asked, experiencing a sudden clenching of fear as they pulled onto Professional Drive.

"Just around the bend. There's this gorgeous tree there. It's made for picnics. Tell me if you agree."

Within moments, Shay saw exactly what Liza meant. "Omigosh! That is one awesome tree."

Liza chuckled. "We have to hike in a little ways, okay?"

"Sure." Shay stepped out of the truck and stared at the beautiful mushroom cloud of oak tree. It had to be at least three hundred years old. The trunk was thicker than Shay and Liza's bodies put together. Poison oak had lost a battle with the tree and a dead vine as thick as Shay's thigh wrapped sinuously around its pockmarked trunk.

Liza held a barbed wire fence down so Shay could cross, all the while juggling the basket. Shay stepped over and laid the tablecloth across the barbs, then held the fence so Liza could cross.

Liza smiled at Shay as she retrieved the tablecloth and Shay felt the same melting feeling as before. They turned as one and walked side by side toward the tree.

"Acorns are down," said Liza as a flock of wild green parrots exploded from the branches and flashed away in a blur of lime green color. She shielded her eyes and watched the parrots circle.

"They'll be back," she said, "and will give us hell for disturbing them, I bet."

Shay was eyeing the tree mistrustfully and Liza laughed at her.

"We'll sit a little way out," she said, setting the basket aside and taking the tablecloth. After kicking acorns aside until she had a smooth plane of grass, she spread the cloth and placed the basket in the center. She patted the cloth and took a seat next to the basket.

"Come on! I'm starving."

Shay smiled, amused at Liza's easy manner, her simple joy in life. She knelt and removed the wine and two plastic cups.

"Sorry this isn't colder," she said apologetically as she poured.

Liza took the wine offered and sipped slowly. And sipped again.

"Holy cow," she said. "What *is* this?" She took the bottle from Shay and held it up to the light. Afternoon sunlight warmed itself in the golden depths of the bottle.

Shay laughed and shared her first experience trying the wine at a vineyard in Charlottesville, Virginia. "It was love at first taste. I buy it by the case now, even though I'm not a big drinker, and every year has been just as good as that first one."

"It's amazing. I need the name and address of this winery. And drinking this doesn't classify as 'drinking,'" she added. "This is an experience. I've always liked Rieslings but this one has them all beat."

Shay dipped her head, pleased that Liza enjoyed the wine as much as she did. Soon she had a feast spread before them and they both jumped in eagerly.

As she chewed, Shay's mind flashed back to her painful time with Pepper. Struggling, she tried to rise above the memory, tried to continue to enjoy this one moment of contentment. It was a battle but she got there. A part of her realized that Liza would never complain about Shay's food preparation nor become abusive if things weren't to her exacting specifications. She smiled. She bet Liza didn't even *have* exacting specifications about anything. She appeared too easygoing for harsh regulations.

Watching Liza's gentleness with the shelter animals was the true measure of her character. Anyone who loved and respected animals the way Liza did would never harm another. Shay was sure of this one fact.

Liza was talking about lettuce. Shay came back to the present with a start, upset by her rudeness in ignoring the other woman.

"I do believe this is my lettuce," Liza was saying.

"Well, of course, silly. I wasn't going to try and take it from you."

Liza watched her blankly as she chewed. "Huh?"

"The lettuce. I won't take it back. It's on *your* sandwich, so yes, it's yours."

She screwed up her freckled nose, wondering about Liza's lettuce issues. She had to say, she'd never met anyone with a lettuce fetish before. Was that why Liza hugged her earlier? Because there was *lettuce* on her sandwich?

Liza laughed at Shay's expression. "No, you goose, I grow it. More than likely, this is some that I grew. Did you get it from McCormacks?"

Now it was Shay's turn to stare blankly. "Yes, yes, I did but…"

"That's what I do. I guess I never mentioned it. I grow things, lettuce, carrots, potatoes, peas, beans, tomatoes, beets, herbs. We even have some citrus groves in Montgomery, but I haven't done much with that."

"You grow them?" Shay asked, making sure she'd heard Liza correctly.

Liza nodded. "Have you ever heard of Meadows Produce?"

"Omigosh, you work for Meadows? Everyone's heard of them. You've got to be kidding me."

"No, seriously. My ex and I started the business twelve years ago in Montgomery. She's still there managing things."

They fell silent. Shay had so many questions that she was having a hard time sorting her thoughts into coherent order. "So she manages the business. What do you do?"

Liza laughed as she began to peel an orange. "Swell up with my own importance mostly, at least that what's my grandmother would say."

Shay lifted one eyebrow and held out her hand for a section of the orange.

"No, like I said, I grow things. In the beginning, I did all the research since I've always been a little plant crazy. I never thought about doing this as a career, but doors opened one after the other and I just stepped on through."

"Meadows is big," Shay offered, her face expressionless.

Liza sighed. "Yes, yes it is. And growing all the time. I have to say Gina's good at what she does."

"So she's your ex?" Shay nibbled at her sandwich and licked mustard from her thumb.

"Yeah, for about a year now."

"How is working together?" Shay watched Liza keenly.

"It's okay. We avoid one another mostly." Liza had finished the orange and reached for the grapes. "I wish things had worked out. As the business grew, I…I saw a different side of her. I'm a little driven. She's a *lot* driven."

"How do you mean exactly?" Shay nabbed one of Liza's grapes.

"Well, her idea of a good time was endless cocktail parties. She said she needed to press the flesh to promote the business." She paused and laid back, contentedly rubbing her full stomach. "Not that I fault her. There is a certain amount of that needed to promote a business, especially a new one. Frankly, I was glad she was up for it. I certainly wasn't."

Her voice softened, grew thoughtful. "The more she pressed the flesh, the more our paths diverged. We had no common ground anymore."

A silence fell as both women followed their own thoughts. Liza watched the sky. Though she tried not to, Shay watched Liza. There was something so endearing about Liza's kind smile. Her cocoa brown eyes were so frank, so honest. And in them Shay had seen Liza's pain at the failed relationship. She idly wondered if this was due to continued feelings for her ex or simply because she had failed to maintain something so important.

"So she changed," Shay said finally.

"Umhmm." Liza turned her gaze toward Shay. "And I did. It's like I saw what really matters to her. Fame. Attention. Things I really don't care about."

"And if she came to her senses?" Shay tried to mask the interest her question conveyed.

Liza sighed heavily and poked at a mound of grass with the heel of her athletic shoe. "It wouldn't matter. I've seen a different side to her now. I have accepted that it's over between us. She's a stranger to me now."

Shay studied her, with admiration and new interest.

Liza's eyes found and held Shay. They connected again, as if melding together. Shay felt as if she had stepped into Liza's being. Whispered words fell from Liza. "I'm going to kiss you."

Shay, munching grapes, grew still. She swallowed. "What?"

"Can I kiss you? I've been wanting to all day."

"No. No, you can't." She knew she didn't sound convincing.

"Why?" Liza smiled, and Shay knew her eyes totally belied the rejection. "Don't you like me even a little?"

"I...I like you, but..."

"So, how about a kiss? A little one? A peck?"

Shay's hands set aside her grapes and grabbed the tablecloth on either side of her body, bunching it into two star-shaped piles. "Why?"

Liza rose from her recumbent position and moved close. "Because it's what we both want," she whispered, her breath warmly fanning Shay's lips.

Hunger leapt in Shay and she pushed forward into Liza's kiss. It was a reflexive action fueled by desire, without thought of consequence, without agony. Falling into Liza's kiss was as natural as breathing and just as welcome. As the kiss deepened from a small kiss into a sharing of souls and need, Shay pulled away, her very foundation shaken. Silence fell between them.

"Are you okay?" Liza's voice was intimate, washing across Shay like hot oil.

"No, not really." Reaction had raised dark blotches on Shay's cheeks, and she felt her heart drop. She needed anger. Anger was going to be the defense of the day.

"I didn't hold you down, Shay. I didn't force you," Liza said calmly.

Shay looked down, uncertain, filled with fear spawned from memory. She caught at her bottom lip with her teeth. Pride wouldn't let her back down now.

"You think you're so irresistible." Shay shifted to her knees and started carefully packing up the picnic.

Liza sighed loudly and stood. She moved to one side, arms hugging her own body as she wondered how such a pleasant time could have turned out so badly. Guilt washed across her, she wanted to kick herself, especially as her body still thrilled to Shay's closeness. And her kiss.

Shay, finished with packing up, stood silently, tablecloth folded across her forearm. "Let's go back," she said, her voice even.

Liza studied the darkening sky. It closely matched her mood. She saw Shay's averted face and felt wretched that the woman avowed to feel nothing for her. She hadn't meant to rush her, but it was better to find out sooner rather than later. But that kiss, didn't that tell the true story?

They moved toward the truck in silence. Liza lifted the fence and opened the truck door for Shay, but the motions were automatic, both women lost in thought.

As Liza pulled the truck next to the yellow Volkswagen, she spoke haltingly. "Shay, listen. I didn't know, didn't realize…"

Shay turned to Liza. She looked as if she had awakened from a deep sleep. "Realize what?"

"That you might not be like me. That you're maybe…not into women."

"What?" Shay frowned at Liza even as she pulled the tablecloth close, comforting herself with the fragrance of crushed grass.

"It's okay…if you prefer men. I understand. I shouldn't have pushed myself on you that way."

"Oh, hell," Shay muttered as she pushed open the truck door. "Go home, Liza. I just need some time, okay? I'll see you later."

Liza watched with her mouth open as Shay tossed the basket into the passenger seat of her Volkswagen and sped off along the shelter road, heading toward Professional. She slumped forward, her forehead resting on the backs of her hands where they held the steering wheel. Would she ever understand the way this woman's mind worked?

CHAPTER FOURTEEN

"Chloe's coming to take you to the doctor, Pop. Can you be ready in half an hour?"

Tom looked at his oldest daughter over the top edge of the newspaper he was reading. "You're not going?"

Liza shook her head and speared another slice of banana. "Nope. Her turn."

His face fell and he folded the newspaper, setting it to one side. "Don't you want to go with me?"

Liza, surprised at his child-like tone, quickly realized how out of control his fight with skin cancer must make him feel. "Dad, you know better than that." She studied his face with fond eyes. "I always enjoy my time with you. Chloe does too, and she just wants her turn."

"She's so busy," Tom argued petulantly. "She must resent it."

Liza laughed and tapped the table lightly with one finger. "Believe me, Pop, we'd all know it if Chloe resented taking you."

Tom chuckled and spun his coffee mug from palm to palm. "This is true."

Chloe wasn't a bad person, she was just...difficult. She expected her way always and, to keep the peace, the family allowed it. She was the pampered younger daughter. She truly adored her big sister Liza, however, so, in Liza's mind, it was a good trade.

As if thoughts could materialize, Chloe appeared in the doorway that separated the kitchen from the family room.

"You two are talking about me," she accused. "I can always tell."

As usual, Chloe carried a large canvas handbag on one shoulder and a large briefcase on the other. The weighty items never seemed to faze her however. Liza believed you could put Chloe under a brick wall and her boundless energy would keep the crushing weight balanced high above.

Chloe's long blond hair must have made a recent visit to the salon as her highlights were positively blinding in the early morning sunlight that was streaming in through the kitchen windows. Her eyes were large, dark brown, with a bewitching uptilt at the outer corners which she, of course, emphasized with perfectly drawn eyeliner. Her lips tilted the same way and she always seemed to be laughing at some private amusement. Indeed, sadness was a foreign emotion to the young legal secretary. Selfishness, giddiness, forgetfulness and thoughtlessness could all describe her at various times but never sadness. She reminded Liza of their mother, Sienna. She too had been a happy woman, albeit never one as demanding as Chloe.

Liza tilted her head to one side as she studied her younger sister. It was a strange phenomenon of genetics. Chloe and Liza had received their father's thick blond hair and ruddy, fair skin. Steve and Richard, the brothers, had received Sienna's Native American darkness. Richard and Liza had also received her stocky, sturdy figure, while Chloe and Steve had received Tom's more willowy form. Strange.

"What?" Chloe asked, clearly irritated at the perusal. "Do I have bagel on my face or something?"

Her phone rang, splitting the morning with Beethoven's *Ode to Joy*. Chloe juggled her bags until she could tap the BlackBerry that was her lifeline. "Chloe Hughes."

Liza leaned toward her father. "Go get ready, Pop. You need any help?"

Tom shook his head and rose. "You got the dishes?"

Liza nodded as Chloe slid into his vacated chair, her bag and briefcase tumbling to the tile floor. She signed off.

"Just the office," she explained. "Is he ready?"

"Few minutes. His appointment's not 'til nine thirty. Y'all have time. How's your schedule today?" She, as always, pushed her coffee cup toward her sister. Chloe lifted it gratefully and took a healthy swallow.

"Not enough milk, Liza. Listen, I need to borrow that blue silk undershirt. You know, the one I was so crazy about when we went to New York? I have a club date coming up, and I thought I'd wear it under my black silk shirt, belted. Won't that look cool?"

Liza smiled and leaned forward. "Tell you what. I'll *give* it to you if you do me a favor."

Chloe stilled and leaned forward, her excitement palpable. Liza never asked her for favors. "What! What is it?"

Liza colored slightly but pressed onward. "I met this woman who's driving me crazy. I need to know more about her."

Chloe sat back, her winsome mouth pursed. "It's about time. I thought Gina was going to haunt you forever. Tell me more."

Frowning, Liza retrieved her coffee. "She moved into the Carson place over next to *Mémé's*. I hear that she bought it under another name, and I found out the other night she knows absolutely nothing about Maypearl. Why in the world did she choose this town?"

Liza rose and started clearing the table.

"She says she had family here, but I can't imagine who. Is she lying? Also, she is real standoffish. I know it could be because she's a Yankee." She turned from the sink and pinned her sister with an unwarranted accusatory stare. "She's from DC, by the way. But there seems to be something else, and I was hoping you could do a little sleuthing for me, see what you can find out."

Chloe, taken aback by Liza's unusual vehemence, was silent for a long beat. When she spoke, her voice was slow and measured. "Are you sure she's gay?"

"What does that matter?"

"Well, obviously you're interested. Does she live alone?"

"I've never been to her house, but I think so. *Mémé* says that a man came out and bought the place for her so I don't know what *that* means...this is why I need your help. Can you get on that national database you guys use and see what you can find?"

Chloe lifted her BlackBerry and began typing into it. "Of course, honey, what's her name?"

"Shay..." Liza realized suddenly that she didn't remember Shay's last name, she'd only heard it once, briefly. "Rainey!" she exclaimed, "No, Raynor! That's it. Raynor."

Chloe eyed her distrustfully. "Are you sure? Wonder how you spell it..." She was furiously typing with her thumbs.

"Have you heard of any Raynors around here?"

"Can't say as I have," Chloe responded, still making notes. "So you want a background only, right? I can do banking and financial, but that gets into a kind of gray area..."

Liza snorted. "No, not necessary. I just want to know who she is and why she's here."

"Umhmmm." Chloe paused and studied her older sister.

Liza shrugged and turned from that penetrating gaze, furious with herself. "I know, damn it! I have absolutely no business doing this. I know it's wrong, especially if I want to get close to her. She'll find out someday and when she does, it'll blow everything."

She twisted the blameless dishcloth into a pained spiral.

Chloe cooed with sudden compassion. "It's okay, Eliza Jane. Why are you worried about who she is? Why can't you just get to know her the old-fashioned way?"

"I told you. The mystery."

"Liza, everyone's a mystery, you know that. What makes her so different? What's the rush?"

Liza pondered the question, finally sitting across from her

sister. "I'm not sure, Chlo. I think about her all the time. She's different from the girls around here. They're so predictable. With her, I don't know up from down."

Chloe holstered her BlackBerry onto the strap of her bag. "What is it you're looking for exactly?"

"I guess if truth be told, I'm trying to learn *how* to get close to her. She's as prickly as a milk thistle, but I sense there's a lot of pain underneath. I want to know...what happened to her?"

"To who?" Tom entered the room. He was dressed in a casual tan blazer and jeans with a dark blue Oxford shirt. The pleasant scent of his aftershave filled Liza with a sense of comfort.

"Look at you!" Chloe exclaimed, rising to wrap her arms about her father. "So handsome."

"Yep, he cleans up well," Liza offered, glad to have sidestepped any explanations. "Pop, I'll be in the garden when you get back, so make sure you come on around and tell me what Doc says. Chloe, I'll lay that shirt out for you. It'll be on the bed, so come in when you get back."

"I will. I'll call you later," Chloe said. She herded Tom out the door while expertly placing her bags on her shoulders at the same time.

CHAPTER FIFTEEN

The insistent beckoning of her cell phone woke Shay the next morning. Her first, totally irrational thought was that it was Liza, and she fumbled for the phone with a mounting sense of excitement.

That kiss the day before had kept Shay awake most of the night. She had loved the sweetness of it. She had loved the feel of Liza's sun-roughened lips against hers. And the scent of her. She smelled of new growing things and that scent above a foundation of a woodsy scent that Shay finally realized was sandalwood. Just being near Liza sent Shay reeling off into a sensual world of erotic imaginings. She longed to run her fingers through Liza's shaggy blond hair and found herself alternately wanting to plunder Liza like ripe fruit and wanting to cuddle with her next to the calm waters of Dooley's Folly.

Silencing the ring and realizing that it couldn't be Liza occurred simultaneously. Shay answered cautiously, eyes too unfocused to see the caller ID.

"Good morning, Shay honey. I hope I didn't wake you up. I have horrendous meetings all morning and wasn't sure when I would be able to call." Don's voice sounded wide awake, irritatingly so.

"Good morning," she said, yawning. "What time is it?"

"Eight-ten, why?" His voice fell. "Oh right! I keep forgetting you're an hour earlier. Oh well, nothing like an early start to the day."

"Right. Dee dear, what do you need, calling me at this ungodly hour?"

He laughed at her mock annoyance. "Just to let you know that Gregory and I are coming to see you!"

Shay bolted upright, wide awake now. Heavy hair fell across her face and she brushed it back impatiently. "No way! You're not serious."

"Yes way." He paused to curse at traffic. "Our flight leaves day after tomorrow at six-forty-five in the A.M. We should be there about two. We've arranged a rental car in Mobile, but I have no idea where to go after that. Greg's picking up a map today and hopefully we'll be able to find Maypearl with little difficulty. I'll call when we get close and you can talk us the rest of the way in. Now, what hotels are there in town? I need to make a reservation."

Shay laughed and twirled an enthusiastic curl with her index finger. "You're joking. You'll stay with me, of course. I have gobs of room, and I'll have the beds made up by the time you get here."

Now it was Don's turn to laugh. "Beds? Beds? Only one will be needed, my dear."

Shay clucked her tongue at him. "You guys always move so quickly."

"Oh, stop it. I'm blushing."

"Well, it's a queen bed. Are you sure it won't be too big for the two of you?"

He laughed. "Perfectly appropriate, dear girl, don't you think? Can't wait to see you."

"I'm so excited you're coming. Let's do an early Thanksgiving dinner. We'll have a big meal and I'll invite Liza."

"Ahh, the tomboy. So things are going that well?" His voice developed a worried cast.

"I don't know," Shay said with a sigh. "We'll see."

"I can't wait to hear more details. I'm at headquarters now and have to run. We'll see you late Tuesday and listen…be really careful, okay? Kisses."

Shay signed off, excited about seeing her old friend again and thinking how weird things work out, sometimes. She'd been feeling a little homesick about not having family and friends to be with during the holidays and now Dee was coming to her.

His last admonishment to be careful worried her. Did he mean with Liza? Or was there something else he wasn't telling her? She shook her head, laughing at and trying to disregard her incessant worries.

Sitting in the middle of her bed, she let her eyes roam the bedroom. Boxes in various stages of unpacked readiness mocked her. She flopped back onto the pillows. How would she ever get the house ready in just two days?

CHAPTER SIXTEEN

The air in southern Alabama is often so thick and heavy that walking through it feels like a caress. Liza could certainly feel it today even though it was technically winter, a season that this far south bore no relation to its hardier northern cousin. And for this Liza was grateful; it meant she was allowed to indulge in her love of green, growing things all year long.

She sighed, trying to gather in enough of the still air to fill her lungs, and stood, both hands massaging her lower back. Her pale brown eyes shone with pride as she studied her masterpiece. Verdant, leafy rows of late season beans and peas stretched a quarter mile on her left. To her right were the fleshier leaves of root vegetables—carrots, beet, turnips and radishes. On the outer rows of each side, the cabbages she had planted were now raising their bright green heads. At the very center of the extensive garden, she had placed long raised beds of lettuce and other tasty greens. It was a vegetarian's smorgasbord.

She turned and checked the strawberry plants growing in a shady patch beneath a stand of papaya trees. This was an experiment, assuming that the slanting winter sun would give life to these sun-loving plants in partial shade. So far so good, as each low plant bore plump ornaments of reddening fruit. They would be loaded soon and would need harvesting.

Liza knelt, scrounged a berry out and popped it into her mouth. Yep, another week at most. Now she had to make a firm decision. This smaller garden, planted and tended lovingly with her own two hands, had proven more fertile than she could have imagined. Harvesting the vegetables by herself would be close to impossible. An ever-changing, ever-growing crew of workers tended the huge fields in Montgomery, yet she was loathe to pull any away from those primary fields. That would mean dealing with Gina, and she wasn't in the mood. Probably never would be.

She studied the long rows once more. This experiment had gotten way out of hand, however, and something needed to be done, soon. She frowned and pondered her choices. She needed people. Who would work locally?

A car approaching snared her attention. It wasn't Chloe's red Mustang, but Mindy's copper-colored Dodge Caliber. Surprised, Liza rounded the house and greeted her in the side yard.

"Hey, girl, good to see you." She drew Mindy into a close hug. "What brings you out when you should be home sleeping off last night's shift?"

Mindy's hazel eyes were framed by dark smudges, and her long dark hair was piled carelessly atop her head and fastened with a big clip.

"Can we talk?" she said urgently. "Do you have a minute?"

Liza frowned. "Min, you know I always have time for you. I can't believe you asked." She turned and made her way to the back door, motioning for Mindy to follow. "Let's get out of this heat and get something cold."

Mindy sighed and once in the spacious kitchen took a seat at the table. She laid her keys and handbag atop it.

"Light beer okay?" Liza asked, offering a dark, frosty bottle.

"Mmm, thank you," Mindy replied, twisting off the cap and taking a healthy swallow. "That's good."

Liza nodded agreement as she swigged her own and took the chair opposite Mindy. "So, what's up?"

"It's Arlie…"

"Oh no, what's happened to her now? She get hurt at work?" Liza harbored a lot of subconscious worry about Arlie because she worked with such heavy machinery at the wood yard.

"Oh no," Mindy responded hastily. "Nothing like that."

"Sheesh! Don't scare me that way." She eyed Mindy. "So what's she done now? Another bar fight?"

"Cheated on me." Mindy's heartache was evident in her voice.

"No way," Liza offered with conviction. "She wouldn't. Not Arlie, not the way she loves you."

"I'm sure of it."

Liza shook her head. "No. How can you know for sure?"

"I…I followed her today at lunchtime. I was gonna surprise her, brought her favorite burger and everything." She paused and took in a deep, shaky breath. "She got in this woman's car. One of the rich bitches from the new subdivision…"

"See there? She was probably doing some extra spec work."

"I thought so too, so I followed them to her house and I got out of the car and was going in after, but I saw them in the doorway, then inside the window and they were…were…"

Liza took Mindy's hand after understanding dawned. "I'm so, so sorry, honey. I will personally kick her ass. I can't believe…"

"Will you talk to her, no kidding? I want to know why, Liza. I'm always available to her. I really thought what we had was good, was perfect."

Tears escaped her eyes and ran with unwarranted eagerness along her narrow cheeks. She didn't sob and somehow that was worse, breaking Liza's heart. How could Arlie be so stupid?

"I'm gonna go," Mindy said abruptly, gathering her things together. "I just can't deal with this right now. Talk to her, Liza, and call me?"

"Wait." Liza stood. "What are you going to do?"

Mindy paused at the kitchen door that led outside. She hung her head, a picture of dejection and pain. "Nothing. At least not yet. Maybe when I understand why, then I can make a decision. We have fourteen years, Liza. Fourteen. It seems like it would be hard to piss that away. I want to know how she can do it so easily when it's just killing me."

After Mindy left, Liza stood in the center of the kitchen pondering this new information. Absently her hand fished in the pocket of her shorts and pulled out her cell. She dialed Arlie with the push of a button. Arlie answered on the second ring.

"Liza! Hey, what's up?"

Her voice was overloud so she could be heard above the machine-driven din in the background.

"Hey. What time do you get off today?"

"In about sixty, why?"

"Meet me at Java right after, okay? It's important."

Arlie sounded dubious, but she agreed. Liza signed off.

CHAPTER SEVENTEEN

Arlie was waiting for Liza by the time she made it to The Java Cup.

Nora spied Liza when she entered and held up a questioning hand. Liza nodded, indicating to Nora that she would have her usual iced Americana.

She slid into the seat across from Arlie and simply stared at her until the other woman began to fidget uncomfortably.

"You'll never believe what I heard today," Liza began slowly.

Arlie leaned back in her chair and tried to look tough and unperturbed. "What?"

"That one of my best and dearest friends is screwing up her life, no, wait, she's pissing her life away. That was the way it was worded."

Nora's granddaughter, Sandy, placed the coffee in front of

Liza, and they shared a few pleasantries while Arlie stewed. After Sandy walked away, returning to her crossword puzzle book behind the counter, Liza once more turned her attention to the other woman. "So?"

"So what? I don't know what you're talking about," Arlie said with a scowl. "You've lost me. Not making any sense."

Liza took a deep breath and held the cool plastic of the coffee glass between both palms to steady herself. "She saw you, Arlie. The two of you. She followed you today. Saw you through the window."

Arlie's jaw dropped as she sat upright. All her tough girl demeanor vanished. She was eight years old again, twisting sulkily in the swing in Liza's backyard. "No. That's crazy. There's no way."

Liza felt anger stir. Lying about it was only compounding the problem. "Cut it out, Arlie. You're busted and that's it. You might as well come clean." She leaned forward until their faces almost touched. "What the hell were you thinking? Mindy loves you," she hissed.

Arlie's eyes roamed as if seeking support from the sparsely populated room. "I...it won't happen again." she said, her voice flat.

"Too late. Do you really think you'll get a second chance?"

Arlie's face fell and she looked as though she'd been hit by a two-by-four. Obviously, the thought that she might be held accountable hadn't really occurred to her. "What? What is Min going to do?"

Liza rubbed her forehead with one hand. "Leave your ass, if she's as smart as I think she is. Arlie, what's going on? I thought you and Mindy had a real good thing."

"We do!" Arlie exclaimed. "We did."

"Then why?" Liza fixed her friend with a damning stare.

To Liza's amazement, Arlie's dark blue eyes filled with unshed tears. The large woman sat back and swallowed to maintain her composure.

Compassion welled in Liza, but she knew she had to remain firm for Mindy's sake. "Why, Arlie?"

"You can't imagine what it's like, Hughes," she said after a short pause. "You're good lookin', got a hell of a personality. Can have any woman you damn well please."

Liza's mouth fell open. "What the hell…Arlie, you're crazy. What does this have to do with the price of tea in China?"

Arlie swiped at her eyes, groaning when Liza fell back on one of their pet childhood phrases. "She came on to me, Liza. This big britches woman wanted me, Arlie Russell, giant diesel dyke. Do you know what that means?"

Liza sighed and shut her eyes. "It means she's married, Woodpecker, and is playing both sides of the fence. You're not stupid. Wait, maybe you are."

Arlie angered and puffed up but then deflated before her friend's steady gaze. "I know," she whispered. "It was such a rush, though, Hughes, you have no idea."

"I *do* know, hon. Swear to God. I've been in similar situations. Going for it does nobody any good," she replied impatiently.

"What am I gonna do?" Arlie covered her face with her hands.

"Are you tired of Mindy?"

"God, no!" Arlie blurted out, lifting a tortured gaze. "Never."

Liza sighed. "Well, talking to her is the first step. Maybe some counseling if she's agreeable. I suggest you go home and get started." She rose and lifted her cup. Arlie stood on shaky legs.

"Are you gonna see the woman again?" Liza asked quietly as they stepped out into the late afternoon sunlight.

"No, I was already breaking it off. It was not a long-term thing, you know?"

Liza pulled Arlie into a sideways hug of encouragement. "Good luck, Woodpecker. Just be honest, okay? Mindy deserves that from you. Promise?"

Arlie nodded, eyes downcast.

"Call me if you need anything, hear? Tell Min to call me if she needs to," Liza added as they walked together for a few paces.

Arlie awkwardly hugged Liza back, and they parted, each lost in thought, both imagining and dreading the impending confrontation.

CHAPTER EIGHTEEN

Liza's cell phone rang just as she pulled into the drive. She'd pondered the troubling conversation with Arlie all the way home, so she wasn't in the best of spirits. Seeing a number marked as private further stirred flags of irritation.

"Eliza Hughes," she barked into the phone, sure it had something to do with a Meadows snafu. Like she needed more aggravation.

"Liza? Are you okay?"

It took almost a full minute for the soft, low voice to register.

"Shay? Is that you?"

"Yes, I hope I'm not bothering you…"

"No, no, of course not. I'm sorry I was so…such a bitch. Rough day."

"No problem. I hope you don't mind, but I got your number from Carol over here at the shelter. I was gonna ask her to call you, but she said you wouldn't mind…" Her tone was doubtful and Liza hastened to reassure her.

"She knows me well," she said, laughing. "Besides the Meadows work I do makes my number somewhat public knowledge." Her voice softened, revealing the intimacy she felt upon hearing Shay's voice. "I'm really glad you called me."

"Good!" Pleasure rang in the word. "Can you come for dinner Tuesday afternoon? At my house? My friend Don is coming in from DC with his new significant other. I thought you might enjoy meeting them."

"That sounds great. What time and what can I bring?"

Shay sighed as if thinking. "It'll just be a simple meal but our Thanksgiving, I guess, so I've got the menu planned. Can you come early, maybe one? That way we can eat by the windows to the back deck and enjoy the view. Don't you think that's a fun idea?"

"Absolutely," Liza said, nodding to herself in her truck. "I'm really looking forward to it."

Shay seemed to grow shy suddenly. "Okay then, I…I guess I'll see you Tuesday."

Liza was disappointed that Shay was signing off. "Oh, okay. See you then. Shay, thanks for calling."

Liza studied her cell phone, pressing the save button so she could keep Shay's number. She had forgotten; it was listed as private. Liza sighed.

She sat back and stared at her father's large frame house. She let her mind roam. It felt pleasant to sit unfocused for a few minutes. Her eyes fetched up on an errant growth of trumpet vine and she made a mental note to pull it up or relocate it. The roots were extensive, though, so she'd probably have to let it die. If she didn't, it would burrow under the siding of the house and cause major problems.

A smile nudged its way across her features. The call from Shay had set a deep-seated and totally unexpected happiness into motion. She let herself savor it for a good long while before leaving the truck.

Her phone rang again just as she inserted her key into the lock. Glancing at the caller ID, she sighed. Mary.

Mary Cross and Liza had been best friends since grade school and during those years, Mary had eagerly agreed with Liza that her brother Steven was a total dweeb or a royal pain in the ass, depending on the mood of the day. Then, in their senior year, Mary and Steve had become an item almost overnight. Steve was already working for Bond Insurance over in Fairhope and their marriage right after graduation had surprised Liza and even angered her. She had harbored some hope that Mary would come to her senses before marrying Steve. She often wondered if Mary, who knew about Liza's lesbianism, had married so hastily in an effort to prove her heterosexuality, not wanting people to think she and Liza were a couple.

And it wasn't that Steve was a bad guy. Liza did love him dearly, but he was a typical big brother, whose goal in life was to make both his sisters wish they'd never been born into his world.

Too late now, Mary had finally realized the folly of her impetuous decision, and it was a realization she discussed with Liza almost daily.

"Hey, Mare," Liza said into the cell.

"He's drunk on his ass," Mary said without preamble.

"No way. It's too early. He doesn't drink this early, does he?"

"On golf days he does." Mary's voice was tight with anger or maybe frustration.

"I'm so sorry," Liza answered finally. "I don't know what to say or do to make it better."

Liza could hear her niece and nephew running rampant in the background.

"Will you talk to him?" Mary said, her voice so low, Liza almost didn't hear her.

Liza sighed again. For someone who hated to get involved in other people's problems, she sure was of late. "Sure, I will. As soon as I can. How are the kids?"

"Good." Mary's tone was still morose. "Stevie lost another tooth, and Mason started at Saturday's football game."

"Awesome. He played really well the last game we came to. I can't say I'm surprised."

The two made small talk for several minutes, and then Liza signed off. She didn't take the time to talk to Stevie and Mason as she usually did. The talks with Mindy, Arlie and now Mary had taken their toll, leaving her emotions raw. She didn't have the stamina to be upbeat for the children.

"Hey, Pop," she called as she entered the house. "What did the doctor say?" She sincerely hoped it was good news.

Her father sat at the kitchen table, contentedly munching on a fast-food meal, evidenced by the brightly colored to-go bag crumpled on the tabletop.

Liza smiled indulgently. Her father looked like a hungry teen, guiltily ramming french fries into his mouth.

"Whoa, slow down, Pop. Whatcha got there?" She stifled laughter.

Her father colored. "Chloe stopped on the way home."

"Umhm," Liza said, opening the fridge and pouring a glass of sweet tea. "I see that. Looks good."

"There's plenty here if you want some," he said eagerly, as if begging her to join him in his act of gustatory sin.

Liza did laugh then. "No, you go ahead. Enjoy it, Pop. I'm not hungry yet."

Liza stood against the kitchen counter wondering whether she wanted to return to work out back or cook something to eat. Or collapse in front of the TV.

"So I guess the treatment went well?" she said.

"Didn't have one," her father said around a bite of burger.

"Really." She was curious. "How come?"

Tom shrugged. "Said I was doing so well, he's going to hold off until after the holidays. See how I do."

Liza placed her empty glass in the sink. "Omigosh, that's fantastic."

She sat across from him and filched a salty fry, studying his face as he chewed. "So I guess you're responding well. I am so glad to hear that. No wonder you're celebrating."

Her father patted her hand and smiled. "I love you, Eliza Jane."

Liza blushed. "Aw, Pop, I love you too. You know that."

He nodded and returned to his burger, taking a mighty bite. "I know."

Leaving him to his meal, Liza wandered into the living room and switched on the television. Her restless mind wouldn't calm enough for her to enjoy any program, however, so she rose and re-entered the kitchen. Tom was washing the few dishes that had accumulated during the afternoon.

"If you're settled, I think I'll go down and throw a line into the pond."

"Sounds good," Tom replied. "Take your spray. Alan says we've had a powerful lot of straggler mosquitoes."

"Will do," she paused in the doorway. "You want to come with me?"

"Nope." He shook his head and dried his hands. "All tuckered out. I have a date with an old black-and-white movie."

Liza laughed. "Sounds like a match made in heaven."

CHAPTER NINETEEN

The amount of work needed to get the house in order was daunting. Shay wandered away from the mound of boxes and paused by the high front window that looked out on the driveway. Usually deer could be seen grazing out there this time of day, but the roadway and surrounding forest was strangely deserted. She sighed, feeling lonely and somewhat vulnerable.

Thoughts and nightmares about Pepper's abuse persisted. It angered her that she was forced to deal with the past even though she detested it. Resting her elbow on the windowsill and cupping her chin in her palm, she let her gaze roam as if seeking answers for her dilemma from nature's bible. After some time she realized something was amiss and her cautious nature went into overdrive. What was it? She chewed on a thumbnail as her eyes darted keenly. Perplexed, she finally turned away. Just as she turned, she realized that there was a flash of white at the end of the drive. Overgrowth prevented a dead-on sighting but when the wind stirred, there it was. Something large and white was blocking the end of her driveway.

A gasp tore through her and she pressed her face against the pane as if doing so would allow her to see more clearly. She finally realized there was no help for it; she had to go outside and see to it.

She moved back, terrified, heart racing. She hated guns but really wished she had one for protection right now. Going out unarmed was an act of courage she just wasn't sure she could muster up. But she had to see what the anomaly was. There was no way she could blissfully continue unpacking while the object was out there.

She twisted her hair in a nervous smoothing gesture and glanced around her living room, seeking some sort of weapon. There wasn't even a fireplace poker in this Southern-styled home. Making a face of pique, she stamped one foot. Why *didn't* she have a dog? She felt a major temper tantrum coming on and tried to calm herself using techniques taught by Dr. Frye.

Breathing deeply, she lifted her keys and phone from the hall table and unlocked the front door. Stepping through it was one of the hardest things she had ever done. Her eyes roamed the forest constantly, seeking signs of ambush as she securely locked the door behind her.

"She's in jail, she's in jail, she's in jail," she muttered to herself, a protective mantra that allowed her a dozen tentative steps along the drive. As the drive curved, she breathed a deep breath and her knees weakened from relief. It was a Tacoma pickup, a familiar one.

Liza, obviously fishing, had parked it a little further down along Dooley Drive than she had last time, making it more visible from the house.

Smiling a goofy grin of relief, Shay turned to return inside. After a few steps, she faltered. It would be nice to see Liza again. They'd parted on such strange terms last time, after that kiss. That memorable kiss. Shay had been having a hard time with that memory. Every time she thought of those sun-roughened, warm lips meeting hers, she turned into a puddle of longing.

Almost as if they were sentient beings, her feet pulled her down the drive.

Liza was indeed in a fishing stance, perched on a cooler next to the pond, but she seemed to be uninterested, pensively holding her pole splayed across her lap. Shay watched her for some time, admiring the normally smiling face in repose. It was a strong face; there had to be Native American ancestry there somewhere. The blond hair threw one off, but Shay could see it in the broad cheekbones and the proud nose.

"So, how long are you gonna stand there," Liza said lazily as her eyes never left the water.

"Just admiring the view," Shay said, biting her lip and silently berating herself for flirting.

Liza turned toward her and there was that disarming smile again. "How you been, Little Fluff?"

Shay made a face. "Fluff? Please!" She moved to stand closer to Liza's *The Thinker* pose. She indicated the pole's position. "Won't catch many fish that way."

"Not hungry," Liza replied, lifting an eyebrow and waiting for Shay to catch on to the reference.

Shay did. "Right. For sustenance only. Listen, I was really out of line that day, and I did apologize. Let's just forget it, okay?"

Liza nodded. "Forgotten, sort of." She studied Shay's casual shorts and button-down shirt. "Those aren't jogging clothes."

Shay folded her arms across her chest and watched ducks as they meticulously bathed out in the middle of the pond. "No, I'm unpacking. I need to get the house ready for Dee and his new man, Greg."

"Who?"

"My friend Don. Remember, I called you?"

"Right. I'm sorry. Distracted."

Liza stood, dwarfing Shay, and Shay moved back as if afraid. Liza noticed but didn't remark on it. "Need some help? Fishing just isn't what I'm in the mood for, I guess."

A war raged inside Shay. Should she let Liza into her fortress? She disliked letting others see her neurotic precautions, worried about what ideas they would form in her silence. Explaining was something she wasn't able to do just yet. A scheduled visit could be dealt with but a random visit... Her mind listed her last visual references of her house as Liza waited patiently.

"I guess..." she began hesitantly.

"Good." Liza strode across the road and tossed her pole into the back of her pickup and led the way up the drive. Shay hurriedly caught up, wondering whether she should broach the subject of Pepper. She hesitated, and they were at the front door within moments.

If Liza noticed the number of deadbolts, she didn't comment on them as Shay leapt forward to painstakingly unlock each one. Instead she talked about how she had always loved this estate and how she had often played there as a child. She complimented Shay's landscaping improvements.

Hesitating at the door, Shay quit breathing as a new fear beset her. Suppose Liza *did* want to hurt her? Or perhaps kiss her again?

"Shay? You all right? Did I say something?"

Shay looked up and fell deep into Liza's concerned gaze. She was watching Shay closely, her face mirroring Shay's own worry. The gaze was loving and kind and Shay's fear dissipated like morning mist in sunshine. Shay wanted to kiss her then and it took everything she had not to wrap her arms around the taller woman's neck and pull her close. Disturbed, she pushed open the door and stepped through.

"Well, this is home, such as it is. Make yourself comfortable and I'll get us some of that wine you love," Shay said as she scrubbed her hands together nervously.

Liza sensed the other's unease and was puzzled by it. "Thanks," she said, gently trying to force eye contact. Shay lifted her gaze once briefly, then vanished into the kitchen.

Liza took in the large combined family and dining room with its high-stuccoed ceiling and airy comfort. A large navy blue sofa dominated the room, but two red Queen Anne wing chairs complemented it. A darkly polished wooden coffee table rounded out the seating area.

To the left of the front door was a dining area with a bare, unadorned cherry table and chairs and a large matching china cabinet on one wall and a matching sideboard on the other.

Although the china cabinet was filled with pale blue dishes, the rooms were strangely uncluttered. Liza noticed several packing crates occupying a far corner of the main room and remembered how long Shay had lived there.

Photographs speared neatly on a bulletin board over the tidy desk area snared her gaze. Stepping closer she saw one photo of a smiling older couple, probably Shay's parents. There was a distinct resemblance. The other photos were generally of Shay with dogs, mostly a beautiful, comical boxer. Other photos showed her surrounded by fuzzy collie puppies. In one she had an arm thrown around a heavily beribboned reddish dog with cute, floppy ears. Liza didn't recognize the breed.

"Hey, what kind of dog is this?"

Shay appeared in the kitchen doorway. "Hmm?"

She saw where Liza was and approached cautiously. As if stalling for time, she handed Liza a cold glass of wine. "This is the Riesling you liked."

"Ahh, that's as good as I remembered," Liza said after savoring a sip. "This one here, the one with all the ribbons."

Shay cleared her throat. "That's Candy, or as she's officially known, Star Farms Wayward Wind M&M."

"Wow, what a name."

"Yeah," Shay replied with a heavy sigh.

"What breed is she? She's really beautiful."

Shay smiled and reached out one hand to touch the photo. "Rhodesian Ridgeback. They're an awesome breed. So intelligent."

Liza peered closely at the photo. "She looks spirited too."

"Oh yes, very. But a good girl."

Liza looked at Shay. "You showed her, didn't you?"

Shay shook her head. "Not really, only in a pinch. I trained her. My friend Carter was her handler."

"That is so cool. Now I finally know a little something about you." Liza studied Shay with amused eyes.

Shay became defensive. "What do you mean? You know just about everything there is to know."

"Like hell! You have to admit, you're a little overcautious. I didn't even know you trained dogs."

Shay shrugged. "It's not important. It just never came up."

Liza's jaw dropped. "Shay? Remember the day at the shelter? Can you think of a better opportunity to mention it?"

Shay fluttered one hand, dismissing the issue, yet she bristled angrily. "Look, did you come here to argue or to help me get ready for guests?"

Liza grinned a disarming grin and placed her wineglass on the desk blotter. "Shay, anything for you, honey. Just tell me what you need me to do."

Pale skin still flushed with anger, but smiling, Shay set her own wine aside and led Liza down a short wide hallway to a large bedroom. It was simply furnished, with a large queen-sized bed, unmade, and a mirrored bureau and tall chest of drawers.

"This is nice," Liza commented, studying the room with appreciation. "I like the light in here."

She noticed suddenly that each of the two large windows had a delicate filigree of wrought iron on the outside. She made a mental note to check for an alarm panel by the front door. She hadn't noticed earlier.

"I thought we'd make the bed and fluff things up a bit," Shay said, her small teeth pulling at her bottom lip.

"Sounds good. I really like this beautiful quilt too," she said, pointing to the stacked linens at the foot of the bed. Determined to put Shay at ease, Liza kept up a constant stream of easy chatter as they worked. She rambled on about helping her grandmother make a quilt when she was younger. Gamboling thoughts plagued her, though. What horrible event had happened to Shay?

As they made their way back to the front of the house, Liza, with new awareness, peered into each of the open rooms they passed. Sure enough, each one had windows barred on the outside. Why hadn't she noticed it from their approach along the drive? She realized then that the filigree panels were so delicate that they added to the overall exterior rather than appearing like the protective bars they actually were. There *was* an alarm panel by the front door, as well as the four deadbolts on the actual door. The sliding glass doors, a true vulnerability, had an outer cage of wrought iron as well as a thick burglar bar on the inside.

Liza felt a pressing need to know what Shay feared but

was afraid to broach it with her. She didn't want to set off that Irish temper again, preferring to spend quality time with the enchanting woman.

"This one is Hattie," Shay said, quietly drawing Liza's attention. She stood by the bulletin board, holding Liza's glass of wine.

Liza approached and took the glass from Shay's hands. She finished the wine in one gulp as she studied the photo. "She's beautiful. You loved her a lot, didn't you?"

Shay nodded and a huge tear rolled slowly along her cheek. Late day sunlight streaming in through the western dining room windows caught the tear and made it into a sparkling diamond. The sight broke Liza's heart.

"Oh, Shay, honey, please. I can't take it if you cry," Liza said gently. She placed her empty glass on the desk and took Shay's hands in hers. She leaned forward and kissed the salty tear away, following its path down to the corner of Shay's pale lips. She leaned back and found Shay's gaze upon her.

Without warning, Shay's arms were around Liza's neck, her hands entwined in Liza's thick hair and their eyes locked, just inches apart. Shay's pleasant coconut scent engulfed her. It was too much. Liza's whole body lurched into combustion and her brown eyes smoldered.

CHAPTER TWENTY

Shay saw the need appear in Liza's gaze and a thrill went through her body. This woman wanted her badly. That desire hit Shay below the belt and she felt a quicksilver pool suddenly form there. Her own desire caused her to stop breathing, and she moved her form sensuously against Liza, enjoying the taller woman's gasp of surprise.

Liza held the firmness of Shay's runner form close and Shay felt her knees weaken. Liza's hands came around to cup Shay's small bottom and pulled their bodies even closer. Only then did Shay allow her lips to touch Liza's. The kiss transported both women to a new place, a cocoon of rampant desire. Liza's hands moved up to smooth through Shay's long hair, the strands thick and silky. Her fingers were hypersensitive as they caressed Shay's long white neck and jaw. Her lips followed her hands, then returned to find the warm energy of Shay's mouth which ignited Shay anew.

Shay's hands wandered under Liza's T-shirt and over her sports bra, finding full, firm breasts, their nipples rigid with need. Her hands moved around and caressed the hard musculature of Liza's back. She sighed. Liza felt so good.

Another, powerfully penetrating kiss weakened Shay's knees, and she felt that if Liza weren't holding her she would fall. She pulled away, tugging Liza with her and led the way down the hall. At her bedroom door, she paused in a moment of trepidation. Making her mind up, she pulled Liza's shirt over her head, mussing the short blond hair. She chuckled and combed the hair into place with her fingertips. Liza's eyes were at half-mast and her breathing heavy.

"I knew you'd be the one," Shay whispered as she studied Liza's dear face.

Liza nodded. "I'm the one," she whispered against Shay's mouth before taking possession again.

They undressed slowly, Liza enjoying the gradual revelation of Shay's small form. Freckles followed tan lines, but her breasts and bottom were like white clouds in a summer sky. Reverently, Liza reached to touch the whiteness, sure she'd never seen such purity before. Oddly enough, a dark blue tattoo of a lizard stretched diagonally across her pale lower stomach. Seeing Liza's interest, Shay covered it with her hand, her mouth growing grim. Knowing that now was not the time to comment, Liza moved close and took Shay into her arms.

Shay ran her hands across Liza's broad shoulders, fingers lingering as if enjoying the planes and curves usually hidden by clothing. Her palms teased at Liza's hard nipples and Liza closed her eyes and moaned. Encouraged, Shay smoothed her hands along Liza's tight waist and suckled gently, first one breast, then the other.

"Oh God, no you don't," Liza murmured as she pulled back and maneuvered Shay onto the bed. Her gentle touch was everywhere. Her warm lips would leave Shays mouth to worship her body, then come and plunder anew, leaving Liza weaker and more aroused each time. Soon Shay was whimpering with need.

She pulled Liza's hand low, pressing herself against Liza's palm, seeking release from the torment of her desire. Liza pushed rhythmically in response to Shay's innate movements for some time. Then her fingers slipped easily inside, going deep and pressing upward. Shay exploded. The orgasm ripped through her and from its power, Liza imagined she could see Shay actually leave her body and then rain back into herself. Shay cried then, great, tearing sobs that she could not seem to stifle.

"Oh, honey, oh babe, please, sweetheart, don't." Liza pulled her close. Her foot flipped up the blanket folded at the foot of the bed and she snuggled Shay, warming them under the blanket. She murmured soothing words and kept kissing Shay's face and hair until the smaller woman quieted into soft hiccups.

"I'm sorry," Shay managed finally, wiping her face with her hands. "I'm such a fool and it's been so long…"

Liza reached and brought her T-shirt around to dry Shay's face. "Here, blow," she said, holding the shirt over Shay's nose. Shay laughed then, the sound shattering her heart into shards of joy. Shay took the shirt and mopped her face and nose, then tossed it aside. Within seconds, she had flipped Liza and was sitting astride her, her wet center pressing onto Liza's stomach. She took Liza's arms and stretched them over the woman's head, holding her prisoner. Shay gently ground herself into Liza's stomach, gasping each time the sensation overloaded. "God, you feel so, so…" she said.

Liza was watching Shay with amused desire. She grinned. "Kiss me, Shay. I want you."

Shay obliged, leaning forward to pillage Liza's mouth. Her breasts grazed Liza's and as the kiss progressed, Liza felt as if each thrust of Shay's tongue in her mouth melted her further into the bed. She pushed her body into Shay, frustrated by her inability to pull her close. Shay shifted her thigh, pressing it between Liza's legs, and her lips moved to Liza's breasts, suckling and nipping gently. Liza cried out from the sensation this spawned, and Shay's lips smiled against her skin. Freeing Liza's arms, Shay moved lower until her lips and tongue found Liza's flat belly. She played there for some time as her hands tweaked Liza's breasts. Liza pressed upward with need, and

Shay's tongue easily penetrated Liza's softly furred folds to flick against her clit.

Liza stilled and the only sound was her harsh breathing.

"You like that?" Shay teased as she pulled her mouth away. Her fingers slid inside and she explored the slick walls within Liza.

"Oh yes," Liza murmured.

Shay's tongue found Liza again and too soon it was over. Liza cried out and her inner walls clutched and throbbed on Shay's hand. Shay's mouth moved to luxuriate across Liza's muscular thighs as her fingers splayed inside, as if enjoying the final pulsations of passion.

Later, Liza moved their bodies into a horizontal curve across the bed and pulled the blanket over them.

They studied one another with new eyes, knowing that a bond had formed. Liza, still basking in the glow of their lovemaking, watched as Shay's usual anxiety began to rebuild itself.

"How did we get here?" Shay moaned, hiding her face in the blanket.

Liza, now alert to the nuances of Shay's fear, tried to reassure her. "It's gonna be okay, sweetheart. You know this was meant to be, don't you?"

Shay lifted fearful eyes and finally nodded. "No one has ever felt so right before," she whispered.

They lay quietly dozing until a towhee's loud call outside the window roused them.

"You need to go," Shay said sharply, sitting up in the bed.

Liza rolled onto her back and looked up at the bed-tousled redhead. "Do you know how gorgeous you look right now?"

Shay smiled slightly but persisted. "You need to go."

"But I want more," Liza said, reaching for Shay.

Shay leapt from the bed and slipped into the bathroom. "No, you don't understand. If anything happened to you…"

Liza pulled on her damp shirt and followed Shay, who was returning to the bedroom as she shrugged into a robe. They almost collided.

"Shay? What would happen to me, honey? You need to explain," Liza said calmly. "What is it you're afraid of?"

Shay studied Liza's face and one hand came up to caress her cheek. Her eyes were warm sapphires. "I knew it that first day, you know."

"You did? What did you know?" Liza's smile was cajoling and sweet.

"That you'd be my undoing."

"How so?"

Shay turned away. "I tried not to care, not to love you, but it's impossible."

Liza pulled Shay close and stroked her hair. "Love is a good thing, Shay. Together we'll work through whatever is scaring you. Trust me, okay?"

Shay nodded and moved away. "You need to go, though. I need to think. All I know right now is that if anything happened to you…I couldn't go on. It would kill me, Liza. It really would."

Liza saw that conviction in Shay's gaze. "You really want me to go, Shay? Wouldn't it be better if I stayed a while longer? I don't want to leave you upset."

"I'll be okay." She tried to smile, but it was a weak effort. "Seriously."

Liza pulled Shay back into her arms and sighed. "Okay. I'll go. Pop's probably sending Sheriff Lyles out to find me as we speak."

Shay smiled for real this time and entwined her arms around Liza's neck. "I'll miss you, though," she whispered against Liza's lips.

Liza's kiss was filled with all the gentleness and sweetness she could muster. She knew that anything more would land them back on the bed. Breaking away, she hurriedly scrambled into her clothing. "Will you call me later, just to talk?"

"I will. I would like that."

Liza eyed Shay. "You know you can tell me anything, right?"

Shay nodded. "I know."

They walked silently to the front door. Shay opened it and Liza stepped through. Turning to face Shay, she laid one palm against Shay's cheek. "See you Tuesday?"

Shay nodded and blowing a kiss, gently pressed the door closed.

Liza listened as all four deadbolts turned before starting down the drive. She looked back once and saw Shay watching from a small window set high next to the door. They waved to one another.

Liza missed her already.

CHAPTER TWENTY-ONE

After seeing Liza walk along the drive, Shay double-checked the locks and made her way to the kitchen, flicking on lights as she progressed. Realizing she was hungry, she opened the fridge and stared inside. Nothing appealed so, after many long minutes, she let it slide closed. Leaning her spine against the cool door, she wrapped her arms around herself and allowed her time with Liza to replay in her mind. She wanted so badly to trust Liza.

No. She mentally checked herself. It was not about Liza, it was about learning to live an unafraid life. Or so Dr. Frye would say. She had a sudden urge to call Dr. Frye and let her know about this monumental accomplishment but realized it was late and her office had closed. She could leave a message but just didn't have the gumption. She was too busy enjoying the glow engendered by Liza's loving touch.

Shaking off the spell she was under, she laughed low in her throat and moved to the pantry. Nothing appealed there either, so she settled on a big apple from the sun-shaped bowl on her bar. She carried it across the living room and settled in front of her laptop. It sprang to life when she opened the lid, and she quickly accessed the Internet via the wireless router. Hesitating only a moment, she typed in Liza Hughes.

After scrolling through an annoying wealth of information about Liza Minelli and her ex-husband, she discovered Liza's serene gaze looking out at her from a 2002 press photo in which Liza and a beautiful ebon-haired woman were accepting a community service award for providing food for a local after-school program. Shay spent a good while studying Liza's ex-partner, Gina Morrow. She was an attractive woman, no doubt about that. She resembled the *Friends* actress Courteney Cox, with a lean face and abnormally dark, sleek hair. *And Liza gave her up*, she thought to herself. Amazing.

Intrigued, she started reading everything she could find about the candidly adorable Eliza Jane Hughes. It was all good. Liza had been involved in charity work even before teaming up with Gina in the early nineties.

Shay leaned back finally. She couldn't find one negative item about Liza. Or Gina, for that matter. This gave her plenty of food for thought, and she chewed on the apple just as earnestly. Could she trust Liza? Maybe so. That still left the problem of Pepper. What would happen once Pepper was out of jail, about three years from now? Would she come looking for Shay? Now Pepper had another target, someone Shay cared about that she could destroy.

She had witnessed Pepper's spiteful anger on too many occasions and so had ample reason to worry. What would she do to Liza? Would she hurt her as she had hurt Shay?

Shay stopped chewing and swallowed nervously. Suppose she turned that blue-eyed charm on Liza? Suppose she seduced Liza away?

Shay stood and paced the living room nervously. That would be the ultimate revenge. Take away, again, what Shay cared for.

Filled with sudden worry, Shay sped back to the desk and

did what she had done so many times before; she typed her own name into the computer search window.

Although there were numerous references and photos, none told where she was currently located. Everything she saw still referred to her simply as award-winning Washington, DC dog trainer and she liked that just fine.

One recent article, a *Washington Post* piece, had a small, below the fold article, asking what had happened to Candy's hard shell. *Silly headline*, she muttered as she perused the article. It bore conjecture only, such as rumors of drug use and a sudden fear of dogs. Rubbish. The articles covering the somewhat sensational court case were the ones she feared most. If one of those nosy writers wanted to get radical, Shay was sure he could ferret out her whereabouts. She sighed. She had covered her tracks as well as she could.

Few people knew about her Uncle Stamos who had lived outside Maypearl in a log cabin amid the bald cypress groves of the Alabama bayou. The Raynor family had visited only twice in Shay's lifetime and that on the way to somewhere further west. Her mother's brother had been a strange man with a limp and shocking, frizzy red hair poking out in all directions. Shay had been fascinated because some of that hair sprouted from his ears and nose. He didn't work, other than prowling the bayou and trapping, and Shay had loved hearing the tales he told about capturing each of the dried, stuffed animals that decorated the walls of his cabin.

Thinking back on it now, Shay realized that her hermit-like Uncle Stamos had been an embarrassment to her mother. Not that Gertie Raynor ever showed this; her manner with Stamos had been full of kindness, tempered with a loving tolerance during his fitful, periodic rants. The mature Shay could see that his behavior was far from society's norm; she now knew it stemmed from a head injury. Legal documents discovered after her parents' death had let Shay know that Stamos had been in a debilitating motorcycle accident in the early sixties. He'd never recovered fully and, much changed, had left the family and headed south, retreating into a bayou cabin built with his own two hands.

As far as she knew, she'd never mentioned Stamos to Pepper or even mentioned southern Alabama to her. They'd talked about visiting Jamaica once but little else about traveling. That was good and as long as no reporter searched out Shay and revealed it to those who remembered her, the likelihood that Pepper would find her was slim. And now that Stamos had passed away, his cabin returning to the wildness of the bayou, the connection to Shay had, she hoped, been erased.

Still. Shay closed the computer and made her nightly rounds, closing drapes and blinds and checking all the locks on windows and doors. She really wished she could relax.

Memories of Pepper's rage lingered, as well as the attitude of superiority that had worn Shay down so quickly. Pepper excelled at finding any iota of self-doubt in someone and magnifying it to the nth degree. Shay never wanted to be in that particular place again.

The fact that Shay couldn't forget Pepper and might not do so for the rest of her life often made her feel suicidal. She knew, deep inside, that those feelings simply had to be dealt with and banished. Anyone with any joy in life, and she had once possessed plenty, could not allow one brutal woman to take it away.

Standing in her bedroom doorway, she glanced back along the murky hallway, resisting the urge to switch all the lights back into brightness.

"She's in jail, she's in jail, in jail," she muttered aloud as she touched the pillow where Liza had lain. She pulled the pillow close, inhaling sandalwood, and cuddled into the bed, willing herself to sleep.

CHAPTER TWENTY-TWO

"You are really starting to piss me off, Steve."

"Well, that sure ruins my day, little sister," he replied, his tone infuriating. "I'm gonna run right out and find a church this minute just so I can make amends."

Liza shifted her phone to the other hand and leaned her elbow on the kitchen table.

Rich sat across from her, loading his mouth with cereal and chewing with bovine complacency. His eyes glanced her way every now and then, disgust evident. Once, when he was looking down at his bowl, she stuck her tongue out in the direction of his dark hair. It made her feel better.

"You are simply too stupid to realize what a good thing you have in Mary and the kids," she said with a sigh. "I don't know why I bother talking to you."

"I don't know either," he countered. "Mary and the kids are fine. Now, butt out."

"Fine. Lose your family. I just hope that when Mary leaves your sorry ass, she doesn't take Mason and Stevie so far away that we can't see them."

She slammed the phone closed and looked up at her father who was making an egg sandwich at the stove.

"He's such an asshole," she said, spinning the phone on the placemat.

"And you thought you could talk to him?" asked Tom, studying the task at hand and not Liza.

"I'd hoped," Liza fumed. "Mary called me yesterday and asked me to. It wasn't my idea. Hell, I avoid him when I can."

"Smart move," Rich said, rising and placing his bowl in the sink.

Tom chuckled and brought his breakfast to the table. "You and Steve have always been oil and water," Tom pointed out unnecessarily.

"It's just 'cause she likes girls. He was okay until she came out with that gal in high school," Rich added.

"Shut up, brat," Liza said. "Don't you have a job to go to?"

"No, too early, dumb-ass."

He grabbed a banana from the bowl on the counter and slammed the kitchen door as he left.

Tom rose, sandwich in hand, and hurried after him. "Where are you going?"

Liza could hear his muffled reply through the screen door. He was going to help his best friend, Brady, work on a dune buggy but would be back later to mow the grass, obviously something he'd promised his father he would do.

Another sound penetrated: Chloe's car.

"Here comes trouble," Tom muttered as he held the door wide and stood patiently as Chloe greeted her brother. Moments later, she was in the kitchen. Today she carried only her data phone and a folder. She appeared practically ethereal without her usual baggage.

"Hey, Pop, how're you feeling?" She kissed his cheek as she brushed past.

"Can't complain," he said cheerfully. "I'll see you gals later. I'm going for a little stroll."

Liza grinned, knowing Pop's craving for peace had won out over his familial duties. And his second cup of coffee. She turned to Chloe.

"Hey, chickie, what brings you over?"

Chloe sat at the table and pushed the folder toward her sister. "I got the stuff on Miss Virginia Faith Raynor. Looks to me like she is definitely gay."

Liza let a slow sexy grin of reminiscence escape, and Chloe, ever the quick one, noted it right away.

"Oh, ho. I guess I don't need to tell you this, obviously." She leaned forward eagerly. "Okay, spill it. What happened? All the details."

"Well, not all the details," Liza said as if shocked. "I was at the Folly yesterday and she came down and…"

Chloe's jaw dropped. "You didn't, Liza. Not at the Folly!?"

Liza laughed and rose to get more coffee because she knew Chloe would be in hers directly. "No, goose, we went up to her house. We had a great time, then Shay got sad and I held her and…well, it was fantastic. She fits me like a glove, know what I mean?"

She resumed her seat and passed the cup of hot coffee and the milk jug to her sister. Chloe took her time and prepared the coffee with lots of milk and sugar. Sighing, Liza rose and poured another cup, black, for herself.

"I'm not sure," Chloe mused thoughtfully. "I don't know as I've ever had that. Men are just real different, I think."

Liza nodded with raised eyebrows. "Yeah, you could say that. Anyway, what did you find out?"

"Heck, you probably know more than I do," Chloe said with a knowing smirk.

"This family is gonna be the death of me," Liza moaned, holding her face with both hands.

"Drama queen."

Chloe lifted the folder and splayed its contents across the table. Liza saw several photocopied newspaper clips and several pages of text. She lifted one small photo of a young woman with short, cropped hair and dynamic blue eyes. Her large, toothy smile was engaging and fun loving. But cocky too.

"Who is this?" she asked.

"Great hairdresser, huh?" Chloe said, clearly referring to the woman's blond hair which was clipped into a severe military style. "This is Dorothy Presley Pope. She hurt Shay pretty badly, putting her in the hospital twice. They were together several years ago, and Shay tried to break it off, probably because of the abuse. She moved all the way to the other side of DC, but Pope just wouldn't let it go. This bitch can't take no for an answer. Get this."

She took a deep breath.

"Turns out Shay was this big-time dog trainer, registered with the Westminster group and everything. Pope found out where she was, came to her house one night, and, because Shay wasn't home, I guess, she killed, *killed*, all Shay's dogs, like six of them."

Liza gasped, eyes wide.

"And some of the dogs weren't even hers but were big-dollar dogs that she was training. Some were pets too..." Chloe stopped and perused one of the articles.

"Hattie," Liza murmured, tears welling in her eyes. It hurt her heart to think of the pain Shay must have suffered.

"Yes, I think there was a Hattie mentioned, but it was a longer name. My friend Connie, over at the *Post*, said it was horrible. Even the diehards at the paper were upset about it. The police photographer told Connie he cried when he had to take the photos," Chloe added.

Liza sat forward and pressed her fingertips to her eyelids. "So what happened to Dorothy? I hope they threw the jail on top of her."

"Yep, she's at Rivers Correctional. Not due to appear for parole for another two years. Destruction of property and attempt to commit bodily."

Liza blew out a lungful of air. This certainly explained Shay's rampant fear. If Pope had stalked her once, she might do so again. It was a wonder she hadn't gone crazy. Liza now understood Shay's unceasing fear and certainly sympathized. She also realized Pope was in prison. Maybe by the time the woman was released, Shay would have a better grip on her own personal power and be more unafraid. Liza made a mental vow to support her in this. And to protect her at all costs.

Chloe sat back and sipped her coffee. She watched Liza. "Has she told you any of this?"

Liza shook her head in the negative.

"So, what now?" Chloe asked. "Are you going to tell her that you know?"

"That's a real good question," Liza replied thoughtfully.

After Chloe left, Liza walked outside to the garden and dialed the number Shay had given her the night before. Shay picked up immediately.

"Liza?"

"Hey, I miss you. Can I come over? What are you doing?"

Shay laughed. "Cleaning, of course. Don's coming and I want the house to look at least marginally acceptable."

"He's coming to see you, not your house," Liza scolded gently. She lifted the water hose with her right hand and pulled it out, placing the length so it would saturate the soil along the top of the row heads in the garden. She brushed against a clump of confederate jasmine and the strong, early morning scent washed across her in a pleasant fog.

"Want me to come help?"

"Oh no," Shay said quickly. "I know how much we'd get done. Like yesterday. Remember?"

"Mmmm," Liza breathed. "Won't forget that anytime soon. But, hey, how about a reminder, just in case?"

"You Southerners are insatiable," Shay drawled playfully. "Can y'all wait until this evening? Y'all can come for suppah."

"It would be my esteemed honor, Miss Scarlett, to dine with you this evening. But only if you allow me to bring my favorite pizza."

"Why, Rhett, you are too, too gracious. I would love to try your pizza, and I shall supply the cold, frothy beverage to go with it."

They laughed companionably and, after agreeing on a time, signed off. Liza was troubled thinking about seeing Shay again. How would she broach the subject of her purloined knowledge?

CHAPTER TWENTY-THREE

A simple kiss hello turned into something much more that evening. The veggie-laden pizza ended up warming the kitchen counter as Liza warmed Shay in the bedroom.

A primal hunger filled Shay as Liza's sun-heated hands stroked across her bare skin. Liza's touch was reverent, and she studied Shay's pale skin as if it were encrusted with colorful, mesmerizing jewels. This adoration made Shay feel heated. Much desired. She responded with languid ardor, torn by her increasing need for Liza's passion and for the seductive security of Liza's presence. Her hands found Liza's and pressed the strong, callused palms harder into her flesh. She wanted to feel Liza as deeply as possible. She needed to feel her completely.

Liza seemed to understand. She lifted her dark, expressive eyes to Shay's, then fell into her kiss once more, hands pressing and caressing roughly. Liza's familiar scent surrounded her, making her head swim in a good way. She pressed her cheek to the slope of Liza's lean ribcage, breathing her in. She smoothed the long, lean planes of the other woman's body with her hands as if memorizing each line.

Liza's fingers entwined with Shay's, and Shay studied the contrasting skin tones and textures, laying the clasped hands on her own white belly. Slowly Liza brought the hands down across the purple lizard tattoo until she pressed Shay's fingers into the pale golden curls at the apex of her thighs. She pressed the fingers there rhythmically until Shay gasped. With a final reassuring press, she left Shay's hand there so both her hands would be free to explore.

She cupped Shay's breasts and suckled them slowly. She took her time, releasing one breast before capturing the other with her soft, scorching lips. She placed her muscular thigh across both of Shay's thighs, pressing her moist center just below Shay's hip as she lay half across the smaller woman.

Shay felt Liza's hot mouth suckling her and felt her mind drift away. She couldn't identify her new destination; it was as if she floated high above both of them, unchained and detached from the earth below. From that vantage point, she could see that the only things holding her spirit to her body were the crimson tentacles of pleasure emanating from and spreading across her passive form. She could see Liza's muscles in the sleek, golden thigh and arm across her, and she took a moment to admire them amidst the crimson, accepting that they further helped prevent her ascent into space. Her own right hand moved across the bright, swelling mound of her sex, moisture rising in tentacles of blue. Every circle formed by her pressing fingers released more blue tentacles into the air to combine with the crimson ribbons around both of them. The color shrouding them was becoming a regal purple.

"I can see them," she murmured, finding her voice with some difficulty.

Liza was breathing deeply, her breath warm against Shay's neck. "What, baby? What do you see?" she said softly. She studied Shay's closed eyes, as if marveling at what thoughts might be birthing behind them.

"Hold me down, Liza," she whispered, using both arms to shift Liza's weight atop her. She felt more grounded then, and she eagerly pulled Liza's lips forward to feast upon hers.

Liza pressed their hips together, pushing herself into Shay. Shay responded with thrusts of her own, eventually wrapping her legs around Liza's hips to bring them as close as possible. Liza reached down and stroked Shay firmly, four fingers and palm entering easily. She watched Shay's face as she pressed into her, enjoying the play of emotions that crossed her features. Liza pressed repeatedly until Shay was just crossing the threshold of orgasm, her mouth open and face rigid with need.

Liza brutally drew her hand away. She lifted her weight off Shay, kneeling between the speckled, alabaster thighs.

"Strawberries," she whispered as she leaned into the feast spread before her. Her tongue meandered slowly, then flicked against Shay's throbbing clit, once to tease, twice to agonize and thrice to energize. Shay grabbed Liza's shoulders and held them with surprising strength. Liza looked up and found Shay watching her, blue eyes blazing.

"Fuck me," she said, her voice brooking no protest, no alternative.

Liza smiled. The woman *was* fierce. Liza knew she could be just as fierce. Kneeling and grasping Shay's leg, she flipped her onto her stomach and, reaching around her waist with her left arm, pulled Shay's sweet, rounded bottom against her own hips. Her right hand found Shay's passion-slicked folds from the front, fingers pulsing against her clit. Her face was buried in Shay's abundance of hair; her breast tips found excitement on Shay's smooth back. They moved together until Liza's other hand roamed down behind and found a home inside Shay's wetness. She shifted slightly sideways so she could go deep and hard, and Shay stopped breathing. She stilled for a moment. But only for a moment. Then she was pushing her entire body onto Liza's arm, her vocal sounds strange and wonderful and raising a fever in Liza. When Shay came, Liza felt it as a jolt through her own clit. Pressing her thighs together, she found her own orgasm as they collapsed together into a panting, glistening pile of satiation.

"Oh...my...God," Liza said sometime later, when her heart had skipped just about enough and had settled into a normal rhythm. "I think I've died and gone to heaven."

Shay, nestled into Liza's curved form, sighed and pushed her heavy hair back from her face. She twisted so she could press a soft kiss to Liza's swollen lips. "I hope there's pizza here in heaven," she said, "'cause I'm starving."

Liza groaned. "So you're telling me you've worked up an appetite? For pizza?"

Shay laughed and slowly rose, pulling Liza from the bed. "One feast at a time, sweetheart. Let's not be gluttons."

CHAPTER TWENTY-FOUR

Leaving Shay in the wee morning hours had been tough, but Liza wasn't up to explaining the new relationship to her father just yet. Plus she'd have to listen to crap from Rich. Few could fail to notice the beaming smile of satiation she wore Tuesday morning, however. Or her excellent mood.

She rose early and, wearing only a muscle shirt and obscenely short shorts, retreated outside just as the sun layered heat and light into the dewy wetness of her garden. She absolutely loved this time of day. Even though she'd had little rest the night before, the dawn energized her. As did her new relationship with Shay. She wondered when they'd fallen in love. Could she define it, explain it? She shook her head as she weeded a row of Italian green beans. There was no explanation. The sensual and spiritual connection they'd forged went beyond words. Trust was a big aspect of it, and Liza knew now how much she trusted Shay with her heart. Her only hope, and it was a hope that grew each time they were together, was that Shay would come to trust her just as much.

The weeds were sparse today and she was glad to see it. The fecundity of spring's new growth had finally eased a bit. The beans, however, were getting a good size on them and would be ready in little more than a week. She looked around after checking the rest of the row. The garden stretched from the orchard all the way to the house, almost a mile of orderly greenery. She realized suddenly that she couldn't even weed it all herself. It was a real worry that had begun to nag at her just a little bit. Still she was very proud of what she'd wrought.

Eagerly she leapt back into her work, weeding, hoeing and clipping overgrowth as completely as possible. Several hours later, invigorated instead of tired, she paused and decided it wasn't perfect but would certainly do. She was done for the day. She stepped out of the growing heat and into the coolness of the kitchen.

"Well, good morning, early bird," Tom said. He stood over the coffeemaker looking not quite awake.

Rich stood at the refrigerator, looking undecided.

"Y'all want me to cook breakfast?" Liza asked.

Rich looked at his sister and made a face of disgust. "Yuk, you're filthy. And go put some clothes on, why don't you?"

"I'll take care of him, Liza, go ahead and clean up," Tom told her, as he playfully slapped at the back of Rich's head.

Later, after she'd showered and dressed for the day, Tom noted her good mood. His reaction was to smile more broadly himself, albeit with a confused expression. They made small talk until Liza realized she needed to tell him that she wouldn't be home for dinner again.

"Umm, Pop," she began at breakfast as soon as Rich retreated to his bedroom. "You know I met this new friend, Shay, right?"

Tom leaned back in his chair, donning his thoughtful face. He nodded.

"Well, she has these friends coming in from DC today and

wants me to meet them at dinner tonight. You okay with that? I really hate leaving you…"

Tom smiled and leaned forward. He placed his large hand over Liza's. "You know, asking you to come here and live wasn't meant to subject you to a life in prison, Liza, taking care of me day after day and forgetting about yourself. I *want* you to have your own life."

"I know, Pop, but I worry you might need something or get nauseated from the treatments again."

He shook his head. "The worst of that's over, honey. You know that. Besides, Rich is off tonight. It'll be guys' night in. Go. Have fun."

Liza patted his hand with her free one, her thoughts drifting to seeing Shay again.

"By the way, is Shay what's making you so happy lately?" He cocked his head to one side, his blue eyes gentle.

Liza dropped her eyes, trying not to blush. "Yeah," she said, "she's pretty great."

"I'm glad, pumpkin. It's time you moved on, had someone special."

She studied him then, remembering that he was alone now. "I wish Mom was still here," she whispered. "I miss her so much this time of year."

Tom sighed. "Me too. She is proud of you, you know. You've accomplished so much and you're just a downright good person. That meant so much to her."

Liza couldn't answer because a huge knot had formed in her throat. She blinked her eyes and nodded, letting him know she'd heard.

CHAPTER TWENTY-FIVE

"You're not serious," Liza looked up at Carol and Chris, her expression incredulous. "This one?"

Carol shrugged. "'Fraid so. Her name is Peaches."

"Peaches." Liza turned critical eyes and studied the young shelter dog that Shay had fallen madly in love with.

She was a boxer mix, true, but that's where breed semblance ended. Her coat was short and smooth like a boxer's but was a strange pale color, lighter than the normal fawn. Her belly and wide chest were white, further adding to the paleness. She was elegant in form, with a longer leg and a more slender neck than most boxers Liza had seen, and her tail was undocked and bore long, wispy hair on it. Her wide face was masked with pale brown and had a thin white blaze between the eyes. The jowls appeared less pronounced than those of a regular boxer, but her body size was comparable to most.

The ears were the clincher, however. Liza wasn't sure of this dog's lineage, but she was sure there was a springer spaniel in there somewhere. The tan ears were way too long for a boxer and bore a wealth of wispy curls, as did the tail. Hanging on either side of the blocky muzzle and sad boxer eyes, the ears were more comical than beautiful.

Liza fell back into one of the empty desk chairs and the dog immediately moved to place her front paws on her knees. Liza absently rubbed the silky, strange ears.

"She *is* a sweetie," she said doubtfully. "A mixed-up sweetie."

Peaches lifted her muzzle and tremulously licked Liza's chin, just once, with her wide, flat tongue. She was very gentle, and Liza sort of understood why, of all the pups at the shelter, this one would be Shay's favorite.

Peaches was watching her thoughtfully, her pug-nosed head tilted to one side. Her overlarge brown eyes were intelligent. Liza wondered what she might be thinking about all this interest.

"You're a good girl, aren't you? A quiet girl," Liza crooned as she caressed the dog's long sides. Peaches chuffed in response and ran her tongue across her own moist nose. "Do you want to go live with the pretty redhead?"

Peaches tilted her head the other way as if giving the matter serious consideration.

Liza laughed and sighed. "Okay, let's get her. But not a word, okay?"

Carol nodded and Chris made a heart-crossing sign on her chest.

Liza looked down at Peaches, who had collapsed her upper body onto Liza's lap and appeared to be snoozing. "Man, I can't believe those ears."

Carol laughed and gently tugged the dog's lead. "Come on, Peaches. Back to your kennel, sweet girl."

"She won't try to place her, will she?"

"Who, Shay?" Carol shook her head in the negative. "She doesn't deal with that part, only working them and doing some of the upkeep around here."

"She usually only comes one or two days a week," Chris added.

The three women walked together into the kennel area. Carol handed the lead to Chris with a smile of gratitude, and she and Liza continued outside into the bright late morning sunshine. They paused at a favorite picnic table and sat together facing the shelter.

"What's her history?" Liza asked. The sun felt good on her shoulders and she could feel sudden sweat pop on her brow.

"You remember Mrs. Grayton, over behind the dollar store?"

"Sure, she passed on about a week or two ago. Did Peaches belong to her?"

Carol sighed and tilted her head back to feel the sun on her face. "Yep, from a puppy. Her nephew brought it to her from Tallahassee."

"Umm," Liza acknowledged. She had followed Carol's example and was resting her head on the picnic table to fully feel the sun on her skin, her arms and legs splayed out, her bottom on the seat and her feet on the grass.

"So what's the deal with you and Shay?" Carol asked after some time had passed.

"She's great," Liza said. "Amazing."

Carol opened her eyes and studied Liza. "So, do you love her? Or is it too early?"

"Love her so much it hurts," Liza replied.

Carol frowned thoughtfully and nodded, before gaining a new sunbathing position, much like Liza's. "Well, that's a good thing."

"Yes, yes it is."

They stayed silent for more than half an hour, enjoying the peace of the Alabama morning.

"I have so much work to do," Carol said wistfully.

"Me too," agreed Liza, "and I'm having dinner with Shay and some of her friends from DC this afternoon. I need to be over there in just a few hours to help out."

"That'll be nice," Carol murmured.

Liza felt the picnic table shift and lifted one eyelid to see that Paul had joined them, splayed comfortably next to his wife.

"Man, it's a nice day," he offered.

CHAPTER TWENTY-SIX

Liza arrived at Shay's several hours later bearing two bags of ice as bidden, a bottle of blended blush wine, plus a big bunch of new asparagus from her garden. She had gone home to shower once more and dress for the evening and felt confident in her nicest jeans, dark blue shell and sky blue overshirt. She had even removed her usual small silver rings from her ear lobes and inserted longer gold dangles.

Shay noticed immediately and Liza could see the appreciation in her gaze. "Well, someone got some sun today," she said, touching Liza's ruddy cheeks. "I think your hair is even more blond than usual."

Liza laughed, placed the ice in the kitchen sink and drew Shay into her arms. "It's just clean, baby, that's all." She kissed Shay and felt her body swell as she inhaled the other woman's characteristic scent.

Shay entwined her hands into Liza's hair and pressed her

body close. Her kiss deepened and Liza felt longing sear through her.

"I want you," she said, breaking the kiss and roaming her hands along Shay's sides.

Shay smiled seductively and pulled Liza into the bedroom. Standing next to the bed, she slid off her jeans and panties in one quick move. She sat on the edge of the bed and spread her legs invitingly. One hand went low and spread her glistening folds in an unmistakable invitation.

"I've been waiting for you," she whispered.

Liza groaned and fell to her knees. She kissed gently along each of Shay's inner thighs until the redhead whimpered. Grazing her tongue along Shay's fingers, she finally probed deeper, her tongue lapping Shay's wetness and pressing upward behind the clit. Her left hand brushed Shay's away, and she held her steady as she plundered the richness before her. The fingers of her right hand penetrated with agonizing slowness before plunging deep and hard. Liza's tongue found Shay's clit again and the slick, muscular walls of her passage throbbed against Liza's fingers.

Shay's hands grasped the comforter on either side of her hips, bunching the fabric, pulling it loose. Her body lifted, pushing into Liza's busy mouth. She stilled suddenly, bucked several times and then cried out her pleasure loud and long. Her body convulsed, inner walls grasping Liza tightly as if never letting go.

"Oh, God," Liza sighed, blazing paths of arousal and need making her feel weak. She knew she couldn't stand, so remained kneeling where she was, her head resting on Shay's thigh. Shay's tightness finally eased so Liza could lower her arms and sink down, but she still held one of Shay's legs with both arms, anchoring herself.

"What time are they coming?" she whispered some time later.

"Soon," Shay answered groggily. Wearily, she pulled up, resting her weight on her bent elbows. She looked at Liza, noting the tortured need in the pale brown eyes. "Come here, baby."

Liza crept onto the bed and held Shay. Shay lifted Liza's shirts and bra, then began feasting on the hard nipples. Every now and then, she would pause and rise to thrust her tongue deeply into Liza's mouth. Soon Liza was gasping for air, and Shay reached into her jeans and brought her lover to climax with just a dozen expert strokes.

They lay spent, but Liza fought sleep. "We gotta get up, honey. What else do you need to cook?"

Shay gasped, waking fully, and then pressed her chest to Liza's. "You make me crazy, you know that? I can't believe I'm acting this way."

Liza nodded. "That's my job, hon." She pressed a kiss to a random patch of freckles that rested to the left of Shay's lips. "Your job is to cook and clean and be my private sex kitten in the bedroom."

Shay sat up and patted Liza's abdomen. "That'll be the day. The cooking and cleaning part anyway."

Shay stood and moved carefully into the bathroom. Liza chuckled and pressed one hand over the crotch of her jeans as she listened to Shay hum while she washed up.

She stood and slowly remade the tousled bed. Coming back to her senses, she grew thoughtful, remembering her ill-gotten knowledge. She realized she had to confess to Shay or it would bother her forever.

CHAPTER TWENTY-SEVEN

Later, in the kitchen, the two women worked together playfully to prepare the dinner. Liza set the table with china that Shay revealed had been used for more than fifty years. It was Noritake china and bore a beautiful spray of pale blue flowers. They looked like blue daisies rimmed in cocoa powder. She turned one of the fragile plates over and saw the design was named *Sonnet*.

"That's appropriate," she murmured aloud.

"Hmm?" queried Shay. She came from the kitchen drying her hands on a dishtowel. "Oh, the china. Isn't it great? My mom had that since she and Dad got married."

"Make me nervous, go ahead," Liza said, gritting her teeth.

Shay laughed. "Get over it. If I were that worried, I wouldn't be using it. Mom brought it out every holiday and birthday and it's still going strong."

"Yeah, but you were an only child," Liza retorted. "This wouldn't last ten minutes in my house. I have two brothers and a careless sister, remember?"

"This table looks fantastic. See, you have talents other than growing yummy veggie things."

Liza lifted a sarcastic eyebrow toward Shay. "I would hope so."

She laid the final fork. "There, all done."

"Good. I'm done in there too. Now we just wait," Shay added.

"Can we talk for a minute?"

Shay looked worried. "Sure. What about? Everything okay?"

Liza nodded. "Yeah, I hope so, I really do."

They moved into the living room and sat next to one another on the dark blue sofa that dominated the room. Liza took Shay's hands in hers and took a deep breath. "This is tough," she said. "And this really isn't the best time."

They waited.

"Just say it," Shay cried suddenly, scowling at Liza. "You're tired of me, right? I'm too pushy, lose my temper too much. Go ahead. Be honest. I can take it." Her mouth grew grim.

Liza squeezed her hands, sorry for setting off that touchy temper. "Calm down, honey. It's nothing like that. I just want you to know that I know what happened to you."

Shay pulled her hands away and mercilessly screwed the dishtowel into a knot. "What do you mean?"

"I know about Dorothy Pope."

Shay stood abruptly, slamming a hip into the high sofa arm in her haste to scramble away.

"How do you know about that?" she whispered, eyes wide in terror.

Liza moved toward Shay and, with gentle persistence, forced the woman into her arms. Shay tried to run away but was tenderly overpowered. She collapsed into Liza's arms finally, her entire body shaking. Liza made soothing noises and caressed her hair.

"Honey, I am not going to let her ever hurt you again. This is not something you need to worry about any more. Please believe me. It's a solemn promise. I will do everything in my power to protect you."

Shay looked up at Liza, reassured by her steady gaze. "You don't understand. You found out about her and me. That means there's nothing that will prevent her from finding me when she gets out. Can't you see? I've done so much to hide from everyone. She's so damned smart, too, so I had to be extra careful. I had to give up everything, Liza, everything. And it still wasn't enough."

Liza cupped the back of Shay's head in her hand and pulled her close. "I know, sweetheart, but I didn't have such an easy time of it. I found out only by asking my sister Chloe, who's a paralegal, to look you up. She has access to records that not everyone can get to."

She moved Shay back so she could look into her eyes. "I'm not proud I did it, either. In fact, I'm ashamed and hope you'll forgive me."

"Why did you do it?" Shay's eyes were shuttered to Liza and it ripped Liza's heart open to see the dejected air.

"I was so...attracted to you. You were all I thought about every day when I woke up until I went to bed. But each time we came together, something happened to mess us up. I wanted to take control, I guess, and just fix things between us."

Shay pulled loose and turned away. Her anger faded. She thought a long moment then sighed. "I can't be mad. I looked you up as well. On the Internet. I wanted to see if you really were a good guy. And you know what? You are a good guy."

She turned to look at Liza and the taller woman grinned widely in relief. "Are you sure, Shay? Are we okay?"

Shay took Liza's hand and pulled her back to the sofa. "Let me tell you about it."

Liza followed meekly, yet eagerly, and took a seat. She waited patiently as Shay gathered her thoughts together.

CHAPTER TWENTY-EIGHT

"I met Pepper—Dorothy Pope—at this new club on the outskirts of DC. Everything was great at first. She was so energetic and exciting that I was...well...overwhelmed. She exhausted me. She worked as a supply officer for the government and worked really long hours but somehow always had more energy then I did.

"I trained dogs then, had a huge business, and she seemed genuinely interested in what I did. I learned later it was all an act." Shay's mouth thinned as she remembered that particular betrayal.

Her voice lowered.

"Things were wild with her. We did things like break through a fence and then run across the Metro tracks with a train no more than a few yards away. Dangerous things. Promiscuous things.

Things I would never do on my own. Over time I've tried to understand why I did these things and especially why I gave her a key to my house. I trusted her, I guess.

"One day I came home from work and she had a woman there, a woman she'd picked up over on Dupont Circle in downtown DC, one of her favorite hunting grounds."

Shay sighed and looked at the hands clasped in her lap. "She wanted a three-way with this woman."

"My God," Liza blurted. "What did you do?"

"I said no, of course, but that made no difference. She told me I was stupid and old-fashioned, then she started sweet talking me and pushing me until..." She stood abruptly and walked to the sliding glass doors.

"Things escalated after that. She burned me with sticks of incense and cigarette lighters. For talking back, she said. She once threw me down the steps in front of the Lincoln Memorial because I challenged her. That one put me in the hospital with a fractured shoulder and ribs. I think the worst thing was when she'd drug me and lock me away. It didn't matter what appointments I had...what clients I needed to meet...what training schedule I'd set up. I'd wake up one morning and be locked away in a closet, listening to my cell phone ring in the other room. The first time it was just a few hours. Later it was for days. I became so afraid that I wouldn't eat or drink anything she'd touched."

She paused and took a deep breath. "I can't even begin to tell you how many clients I lost. I was lying to everyone, even my parents. I couldn't tell anyone." She looked at Liza briefly. "I was so ashamed.

"When I started refusing the women, she beat me more, usually where no one could see. Never in the face. There was one woman I worked the dogs with, a woman named Carla. I showed her once, the bruises, the burns. She ended up testifying."

Shay turned from the glass doors, obviously irritated with herself. "Wait, I'm jumping ahead. The abuse went on for about two years. By this time, Pepper was having to supplement my income just so I could make the mortgage. This gave her so much power over me that it kept getting worse and worse. I started selling household things and jewelry on the sly and saved every cent I could. In cash so she wouldn't know.

"Eventually I had some saved and I sold the house and kennel through a separate postal box without telling her. I had the locks changed when she was at work and then I moved. I went all the way across town."

"Good," Liza said quietly. "That was the right thing to do."

Shay shrugged and resumed her seat next to Liza.

"I don't know. Maybe not. It took her two months to find me, but she did and boy, was she angry."

She turned a keen gaze on Liza. "You know how she found me? By methodically watching at all the malls in the DC area during those months. Especially the pet stores and grocery stores. She was searching for my car, for me. Even though I seldom went out, she found me, just plain bad luck. She hid and followed me home. I didn't know."

She sighed deeply and Liza could see the pain grow. "Then I went to visit my parents for one night. Mom was sick so I didn't take Hattie with me..."

"You put her in the kennel with the other dogs," Liza offered.

Tears cascaded along Shay's cheeks and she brushed them away impatiently before continuing. "I did. Thought it would be a nice visit for her. When I came home early the next morning, I called to her and went out to let her come inside and...the gate was open. Then I saw them. They were so cold, just lying where she'd left them, not even on the sheepskins in their warm little houses or inside the shelter, but on the concrete and in the frozen grass. Several had fought back because they found her blood there, and it helped build the case against her."

"My God, what did you do?" Liza found Shay's hands and held them to try and comfort her.

"At first, I don't know. After seeing them, I...I went out of my head, I think. Don, my friend who's coming today, he lived a few houses down from me. I didn't know him then, but he knew me by sight. He said he found me on his back lawn curled into a fetal position, right on the frozen grass. I was sobbing and muttering crazy stuff. After wrapping me in a blanket—he said I was blue from the cold—he took me back home but saw what had happened and rushed me to the hospital. He called the police on the way, which I don't remember, and he also called a therapist friend, Rachel Frye, to meet us at the hospital. He told me later he knew how much I loved the dogs, just by watching me work them from his back porch deck, and knew I'd need some heavy duty help to get past it."

"Can you imagine what would have happened had he not helped?"

"I think about that every day," she replied, lifting wet, reddened eyes.

"So then what happened?" Liza prodded gently.

"Well," Shay took a deep breath. "After several weeks of therapy, I got *really* angry. I stayed with my parents after they released me from the hospital because I was just too afraid. Dee came to visit all the time and with his help and reassurance, I went after Pepper. My mama was getting sicker and even though we tried everything, she passed the following month. I stayed with Daddy a little longer, but he went soon after."

"I guess everything has a reason. His death gave me the extra resources I needed to hire the best DC prosecuting lawyer around and we brought out the big guns."

"That must have been so horrible," Liza said, shaking her head.

"The whole lesbian thing was a nightmare. My lawyer kept trying to disregard it and say Pepper was a stalking lunatic who would no doubt have killed me if she'd had the chance. Her defense attorney was a tough old bird and he may have won in the end, but she kept stepping on his toes and losing her temper in court. They tried to drag my character through the mud, saying I'd led her on and promised undying love and that *she* was the one thwarted in the relationship. Her behavior in court allowed the jury to quickly make up its mind."

She sighed. "I was never so relieved in my life. I'm just glad my parents didn't have to go through it."

Liza nodded. "The universe just somehow always knows what's best."

Shay squeezed Liza's hand, then rose to look out the window

at the darkening afternoon. "The best part is, all the money she makes in prison has to go to pay the dog owners for damages, for losing their livelihoods. I was glad of that. She deserved to pay. With money *and* jail time."

Silence descended and settled for a long minute.

"I wonder where they are," Shay mused, studying the drive.

As if on cue, her cell phone sounded. Shay strode across the room and eyed the glowing screen. She winked at Liza. "Wanna bet they're lost?"

Liza stood, amazed by the sudden shift in mood. She shook her head in the negative.

"Don, where are you?" Shay asked calmly. She listened intently a few minutes, then smiled. "Yes, we'll walk down so you can see where to turn," she said. "Go around slow one more time."

"Where is he?" Liza quizzed after Shay signed off.

Shay walked to the table beside the door and picked up her keys. "They've been driving around the pond, not sure where the driveway is." She held out her hand to Liza. "Let's walk down and show them where to turn."

CHAPTER TWENTY-NINE

The ease Shay manifested in switching from the painful topic of Pepper onto the brighter topic of dealing with the imminent guests gave Liza pause. She wondered if Shay was forcing emotions away into neat cubicles and not bringing them out to be dealt with fully. She decided to query her about it as they strode along the drive.

"Shay, how do you think Pepper's abuse has changed your life?"

Shay bristled and her reply was brusque. "You see how I live. I'm incarcerated in my own home. I even stagger my jogging days so there'll be no pattern. Sometimes I wonder if I'll ever get over it."

Liza dropped her head, pondering Shay's brittle anger, clearly a protective cloak. "I realize that, and I have one thing to say. I want you to think about this okay?"

Shay paused near the end of the drive and studied the other woman. "Okay."

"It is not up to Pepper how soon you get your life back. It's up to you." She pressed a quick kiss to Shay's forehead. "That's all I have to say."

Shay studied Liza, then smiled slightly and nodded. "Do my eyes look red?"

"You look great. Let's go find those boys."

They stepped onto the asphalt of Dooley Drive and, after a few minutes, saw the slow approach of a champagne-colored Toyota Camry.

"That's them," Shay whispered excitedly, taking Liza's arm.

As the car pulled close, the man driving, Don, as Liza learned later, lowered his window.

"Can we say 'backwoods,'" he said, laughing. "Shay, you need to get in this car and come right back to DC this minute."

Shay placed her hands on her hips, elbows jutting out like triangle points. "Absolutely not and just for fun, we're going to make you tour the single, one-room bank here in town."

"No, no," Don cried in mock horror, "anything but that!"

Laughing, Shay leaned in for a kiss and quick hug. She studied his face, hers mere inches away. "I am so glad to see you," she said, her voice low.

He smiled and touched her forehead with his. "You look great, kid. This place must be agreeing with you."

Shay straightened and motioned Liza close. "Don, this is Liza."

Don and Liza shook hands, exchanging pleasantries. He was older than she had expected.

"Greg, meet Liza and Shay," Don said, leaning back so his companion Greg could shake hands.

"Okay," Don said, "introductions made. Can we get out of this car now?"

Shay laughed and pointed up the sloping drive toward the house. "Right up there, sweetie. We'll be right behind."

Shay took Liza's hand and they followed the rental car in companionable silence.

CHAPTER THIRTY

Don and Greg were both small people, no bigger than Shay, and Liza began to wonder if all DC folk were this size. Maybe a race of fairy people, the Tuatha Dé Danann, had settled there as they had in Ireland. At five foot eight inches, Liza felt like a big-boned giant in their presence. They didn't seem daunted in the least, however, buoyed as they were by a type of high, ethereal energy.

Don talked a lot, wittily. His round head was balding gracefully, and he seemed to have become comfortable with the fact. He did have a thick mustache to compensate, but it was neat and well-trimmed. His large, dark Mediterranean eyes were friendly, and full lips danced across large white teeth as he chattered.

Greg, though just as small, was very different. He had a full thatch of thick, black hair, Asian eyes and a smooth, clean-shaven face. His manner was calmer as well, his movements slower.

"So, Liza, you grow vegetables?" Don said after they settled at the table. "Where's your base of operations?"

Liza leaned to accept the glass of blush wine Shay passed to her. She nodded a warm thank you, meeting Shay's gaze to connect momentarily, before answering. "Montgomery. Meadows owns about two hundred acres there just outside the city proper. We have about forty-five regular employees and use some seasonal migrant labor."

"How in the world does one even start such a business?" Greg asked.

Liza explained the history of the startup as Shay, also listening intently, placed the last few serving dishes of food on the table. Shay took her seat and sipped her wine. When the conversation lagged, she held out one hand to Liza and the other to Don. Don took Greg's hand and Greg took Liza's. Shay murmured a small blessing of gratitude and then released the hands.

"Okay, dig in. I hope you like everything."

Liza gazed hungrily at the food and was amazed at the feast before her. Sliced ham and turkey artfully arranged on a platter was the focal point. Spreading out from that were bowls bearing steaming mashed potatoes, green beans, cooked squash, cornbread stuffing, whole cranberries, asparagus spears dribbled with hollandaise sauce and homemade crescent rolls.

"Wow," she breathed. "I didn't realize all those good smells would pan out like this."

Shay laughed and nudged Liza gently. "Just workin' my way to your heart, darlin'," she explained.

Liza laughed and blushed.

Don watched them, a bemused smile adorning his lips. "So, seriously. Who catered?"

"I did it," Shay retorted. "All by myself. Liza brought the wine and the asparagus. But I cooked everything. I used a great cookbook."

"Well, how about that? See what spending some time with food rather than dogs does for you?" He winked at Shay and continued chewing appreciatively. He glanced once at Liza, then cleared his throat. "Speaking of that, do you have any plans?"

"Plans for what?" Shay sliced a piece of turkey and popped it into her mouth.

"More dogs. Will you start training again here?"

Shay saw the way he was perusing Liza and set his mind at ease. "It's okay, Don, honey. She knows all about it."

"About what?" Greg asked, helping himself to more asparagus.

Silence entered the room as if a physical being. Liza and Don both waited for Shay to say what she would. She hesitated a long minute.

"A woman stalked me and killed my dogs," she explained.

"Oh, that," he exclaimed too quickly, eyes downcast. "It must have been horrible. I hope you sued her ass."

Liza chuckled hollowly, effectively breaking the tension. "Spoken like a true lawyer, Greg."

"Well," Shay began, "she *is* in jail in North Carolina and shouldn't be out for two more years. I just hope she has learned her lesson. That's all I can say."

Liza and Don both eyed Shay, worried about how calmly she was treating the ongoing, crippling fears they both knew about. Don looked at his plate guiltily.

"Dee was the one who found me," Shay told Greg. "After it happened. He took me to the hospital and stayed with me. This guy's a sweetheart. I hope you realize that." She pointed her fork at him for emphasis.

Greg smiled at Don and his face lit with love and admiration. "I do, girl. You know I do." The two touched hands in a brief caress as Don turned his attention back to Shay.

"Okay, Shay, this is important," Don said, clearing his throat. "As much as I like your business at Regional, I need to tell you there are fifteen, *fifteen*, online banks now that pay more interest than we can. You need to choose one and we'll move some funds over, okay?"

He turned to Liza. "And you, miss, do you have your funds in a high-yield checking or savings account?"

Shay and Liza looked at one another and laughed.

"You'll get used to it, honey," Shay told Liza. "It's just part of who he is. Money is his life."

Liza sighed and lifted another roll from the basket. "Hey,

I'm all over making more money. I need tons of investment advice because when it comes to that topic, I'm pretty well lost."

"Most people are," Don agreed, nodding sagely. "Some of us just understand it, while others don't. I'll give you my card and if you ever have any questions you can just call or email me."

Shay glanced at Liza and a special message of contentment passed between them.

"Thank you, Don. I will definitely take you up on that offer."

"Oh my gosh, anybody need anything?" Shay asked, as if suddenly remembering that she was the hostess.

"You've already made my day, Shay, honey." Liza sighed. "This is soo good. I'm going to get unbelievably fat if I continue to hang out with you."

Don and Greg laughed as Shay blushed with delight.

CHAPTER THIRTY-ONE

"So, she told you about what happened to her?" Don studied Liza.

Shay had firmly negated Liza's offer of help loading the dishwasher and shooed her from the kitchen. When Liza persisted, that fragile temper flared so Liza had retreated to the safety of the sofa.

Liza focused on Don, relieved that the subject was out in the open at last. "Yes, she has. We were talking about it before you guys arrived."

He took a deep gulp of cold scotch. Moisture glistened on the glass as light found it. Liza knew he was wrestling with his loyalty to Shay. Wondering how much he should say. And, as could be predicted, loyalty won out.

"So you understand my concern for her well-being." His gaze found hers and locked fiercely. "I need you to be careful with her. She's more precious and much more fragile than you realize."

Liza glanced away from his intensity, her eyes settling on Shay, who was in the kitchen with Greg, oblivious to Liza's interest. They were intently discussing a china plate Greg was turning in his hands.

Liza turned back to Don. "You know, we haven't known each other very long but I have to say, there's no one more precious to me than Shay," she stated firmly. "I'll do everything in my power to protect her and make her life a happy one. You don't need to worry."

Don eyed Liza a long time as if judging her merit. She stared back evenly. Finally, he nodded, clearly impressed by her dedication. "It looks like I might not have to."

He clasped her hand briefly, letting go when Shay and Greg entered the room.

"Dishwasher's all loaded and fine china washed," Shay said cheerily, taking a seat in the armchair across from Liza.

"This looks way too serious," Greg intoned, seating himself next to Don on the sofa and pressing close, eyes bright. He slipped off his loafers and tucked his feet under his body as he perched next to Don. "What's all this about?"

Shay smiled, but her eyes were worried as they passed rapidly from Liza to Don and back again.

Don laughed, trying to put Shay at ease. "Relax, you two. Nothing too earth-shattering. Liza was just singing Shay's praises."

He addressed Shay. "I think she's smitten with you."

Shay turned to Liza as she settled more comfortably into the armchair. "Oh, really. Is there something you want to tell me, El?"

Liza chuckled, embarrassed. She lifted her glass and held its coolness to her lips.

Shay was thrust forcefully back to the early morning hours when Liza had wakened her by decorating her body with ice cubes and proceeding to lick the spaces in between until each cube had melted into a puddle of lukewarm water. The coolness of the ice and the wet heat of Liza's tongue had torn at Shay's senses like hurricane winds. She realized suddenly that she wasn't breathing and that her body ached for Liza.

She took a deep, shuddering breath. "Well, I guess not."

Liza smiled and Don cleared his throat. Clearly, he had sensed the sensual energy between the two women. "So, what's this about a homeless party tonight?"

Relieved by the change of subject, Liza explained about Ro and Kim and the work they'd been doing for Maypearl.

"That's admirable," he said when she finished. "You don't see a lot of that type of dedication these days, especially among young people."

"Hey, the young are often the very first to step up," Shay countered. "Although I have to admit I haven't been as involved as I'd like."

"Ummhmm," Don said with a raised eyebrow. "My point."

"Are we invited?" Greg asked. "I'd love to go just to see what they're doing."

"Absolutely," Liza said. "We're always looking for helping hands. Tonight is the first night they serve Thanksgiving dinner. They serve it every day now until actual Turkey Day."

"Doesn't that use a lot of resources? That's..." he paused to calculate, "nine dinners."

"True," Liza agreed, "but they always have a truckload of turkeys donated by Doc King, so they might as well use them."

"Don't forget the vegetables you donate," Shay reminded her. "El is real big into donations," she told Greg.

"Meadows is, you mean. Everything I do, I do through them. I may be changing that in the future, though."

Shay tilted her head to one side. "What do you mean?"

Liza blushed, reluctant to brag about her green thumb. "Well, I've got a little garden behind the house and it's doing well. Really well. I think my future donations, at least locally, can come from there. Needs to come from there."

"What are you growing?" Greg asked curiously. "Isn't it too hot to grow stuff here?"

"Oh no, it's very temperate. Remember, we're on the Gulf

here so that moderates the heat. This time of year is the best season before the higher heat of summer."

"She must grow everything. Carol, over at the local animal shelter, told me that her donations help keep the homeless shelter operating under budget *and* the animal shelter too. Carol says they wouldn't make it without her help."

"Meadows' help," Liza reminded her gently. She checked her watch. "Well, if we're going to help out, we'd better go now. It's getting late and they'll be serving soon."

After several minutes of gathering essential items, the four waited while Shay securely locked the house. Walking to the cars, Don laughed. "Well, it's easy to see which car we'll be taking."

Shay laughed and slipped her arm through Liza's. "Well, we could go in the Bug. Anyone have a shoehorn?"

"Or you guys could ride on the back of my pickup," Liza offered, trying to be serious.

"Just get in," Don said, opening the back door of the Camry.

CHAPTER THIRTY-TWO

An inordinate number of cars and trucks filled the asphalt parking lot of Recognition Baptist, and Liza wondered if there was a service inside. She wouldn't have been surprised. Recognition was the only Baptist church between Maypearl and Fairhope and had a busy, active congregation.

"Do we need to be quiet?" Greg asked in a whisper as they paused outside the church.

"No, we're not going through the church. The mission is this way," Liza directed, leading the others around to the basement entrance along the northern side of the church. A bank of spicy-scented holy basil on one side and sweet jasmine on the other welcomed them inside.

"Smells heavenly," Don said, brushing the bushes as he strode the narrow sidewalk.

"I think that's the idea," said Shay, chuckling and nudging him.

"Behave, you two." Liza chided, smiling as she opened the heavy metal doors.

Inside the party was in full swing. Festive music sounded from a small portable CD player just outside the kitchen doors. The homeless, mission guests and the staff milled about the large dining hall. The smell of roast turkey and fresh rolls wafted through the room.

"This is wonderful," Shay said. "You mean all these people can stay here if they need to?"

Liza nodded as she led the way to a punchbowl- and cookie-laden table. "Absolutely. The whole back area over there is divided into two big dorm-like rooms that can house twenty people each."

"Are they usually full?" Greg asked. He was glancing around the dining hall trying to imagine the full footprint of the mission.

"I can't even believe I'm eating this after that dinner you served," Liza muttered, chewing a peanut butter cookie. "Usually, Greg, but it's such a transient population that it fluctuates. Sometimes two people, sometimes thirty. When there's a cold snap, it fills pretty fast."

"And don't forget the people who just come in to clean up or get a meal," Rosemary added, coming up behind them. Kim was at her side and both wore Pilgrim hats.

Liza laughed. "Don't y'all look cute."

"Every day," Kim answered smugly, "but I thought you knew that."

Rosemary drew Shay into a quick bear hug, and Liza hastened to introduce Don and Greg.

"Sorry we can't stay and visit guys," Kim said, "but we're going to start serving."

"We're here to help," Greg told her. "Just tell us what to do."

As Rosemary gratefully pulled Don, Greg and Shay behind the serving area and gave them direction, Liza studied the room. More than thirty people crowded the brightly decorated dining room. Most had already found seats at the hodgepodge of donated tables while others milled about looking for seats.

Though she spied and waved to locals such as Doc and Paula King, Doc Huffner and the Jacksons, she didn't see Arlie and Mindy. She hadn't talked to either of them since that day at the Java Cup and was worried about the outcome of their difficult confrontation.

"Liza, you okay?" Rosemary asked, coming to stand next to her. She studied the room as if wondering what had snared her friend's interest.

"Have you heard from Arlie and Mindy?" Liza asked thoughtfully.

Rosemary frowned at her. "No, I called to say hi earlier in the week but didn't get an answer so I just left a message. Should I have?"

Liza sighed. "No, just haven't heard anything lately."

"I'm sure they're fine. Maybe they went over to Seminole to visit Min's mom."

"You're probably right," Liza said, smiling to put Ro at ease.

Rosemary sensed that Liza was troubled, however. "You know, you could call. I'm sure they have their cell phones with them."

Liza nodded. "You're right. I may do that. Have you seen Chris? I need to ask her something."

Rosemary nodded. "She and Tommy were here, but she said she had to do something for the shelter so they took off just a few minutes ago. They're trying to get a place here in town so if you hear of anything, let me know."

"Sure, will do."

The two made their way toward the serving area so they could help dish up food onto plates for the people seated at the tables. A tribe of teen volunteers stood ready, awaiting plates so they could serve as wait staff.

"So, what's the latest?" Rosemary asked, glancing sideways at Liza.

Liza grinned and blushed. "She's fantastic. I can't believe my luck stumbling onto her the way I did."

Yeah," Rosemary agreed dryly. "Trampling my girlfriends is always the way I like to trap 'em."

"Whoa, what's going on over there?" Liza said, taking

Rosemary's arm, halting their progress. She was looking at the food service bar where Don and Greg, behind it, were arguing heatedly. Liza couldn't hear what they were saying because the whole argument was *sotto voce* and just between the two men, but it was clear something was amiss.

"Should we intervene?" Rosemary asked cautiously.

Liza glanced toward Shay, standing ready over by the green vegetable station, and found her oblivious to her friends' distress. "I don't think so, not without Shay's involvement. I know you're worried about the servers but they don't seem affected."

As they watched, however, it became a moot point as both men abruptly ceased arguing and quietly resumed dishing up mashed potatoes and gravy onto the line of plates conveyed along the counter.

Rosemary and Liza looked at one another. They shrugged and donned the aprons awaiting them behind the serving area.

CHAPTER THIRTY-THREE

"Listen, guys, we need to talk."

Don's voice arrested them as they entered a darkened house still fragrant with good cooking smells. Shay glanced at Don in surprise as she pressed the door closed and engaged all the locks.

He took Shay's hand and led her to the sofa. He took both hands and sat her gently down and then motioned for Liza to sit on the other side. Liza switched on a nearby lamp and sat. Greg stood nearby, face ashen, and Liza had a sudden sinking feeling in her stomach.

"I have some bad news," he began gently. "But I don't want you to get too crazy about this. We will deal with it. I don't want you to worry."

Shay's eyes grew wide and her breathing rate increased. "What is it?"

"Rachel, Dr. Frye, is dead. She's been murdered."

Shay gasped. "How? When? How could this happen?"

Don held Shay's hands more firmly as his large eyes filled with unshed tears. "Two weeks ago; someone broke into her office and stole some of her files."

Liza stood suddenly and moved to the bar. She poured several fingers of straight, single-malt scotch and brought it to Shay. Loosening her hands from Don's, Liza pressed the glass into one. "Drink this, Shay. Now!"

Don's wet eyes connected gratefully with Liza's as Shay did as she was told. She shivered once, as the scotch went down, then spoke quietly. "She's the only other person I gave the new address to. My file's missing, isn't it?" She leveled her gaze on Don, daring him to lie.

Don sighed, his eyes tortured. "Yes," he whispered. "Yes."

Shay studied him a long time, her thoughts going back to that first time they'd met. How he had helped her, cuddling her into a blanket and into his arms like a loving father.

"There's more, isn't there?" she said finally. She lifted the glass to her lips and took another, deeper drink. Liza laid one hand on Shay's shoulder, as if bracing her.

"Pepper's out…"

Tears welled in Shay's eyes, then spilled over to cascade along her drawn cheeks. "No, Don," she wailed. "No, don't…"

Don pulled her close and buried her face in his neck. He held her as she sobbed. Liza, her own eyes moist, looked at Greg. He shrugged, portraying his feelings of helplessness. They waited. Liza fetched a nearby box of tissues and sat down next to Shay, setting aside the drink and pressing several tissues into her hand. She handed the box to Don.

"Okay," she said finally. "What do we need to do?"

"Wait," Shay interrupted, her voice muffled by tears. "I want to know how that bitch managed to get out."

Don sat back, mopped his face with a tissue and then scrubbed at his face roughly with both hands. "You won't even believe it. It was damned politics!"

Shay dabbed at her own face, then pierced him with a look of annoyance.

"Really, it's insane. It seems Pepper is a Brit. She was born in the U.K. but has been in the U.S. so long that she has dual citizenship."

Shay nodded. "I know about that, but my lawyer said that wouldn't matter because she'd lived here so long. He investigated that!"

Don rose and moved to his briefcase which was resting against the leg of Shay's desk. He fished through it while Liza wrapped a comforting arm about Shay's shoulders and helped dry her face with the tissues folded in her free hand.

"Here," he said, returning and handing her a small newspaper clipping. "Read this."

Shay squinted at it, finally handing it to Liza. "Please?"

Liza smoothed the clipping and began to read aloud as Don mixed himself a drink at the bar.

Dorothy Presley Pope, a 32-year-old U.S. Government Navy Department supply clerk, who was convicted of aggravated assault with intent to commit bodily harm in 2005, has received a full pardon from Governor Timothy Robinson. The governor said in a statement that he decided to pardon Ms. Pope to prevent her from being deported to Britain, where Ms. Pope was born and lived until the age of thirteen.

Governor Robinson announced today that he has granted Dorothy Presley Pope a full but conditional pardon of her 2005 conviction in order to allow Pope to seek relief from deportation from the federal immigration courts.

Pope has not fully served the sentence imposed upon her for her convictions but has had an exemplary disciplinary record while in prison. In that time, she has participated in work release programs with youth outreach to counsel youth against violence and has become a symbol of rehabilitation for many young people.

Ms. Pope faces deportation under a federal statute that mandates the removal of a lawful resident alien upon conviction of an aggravated felony or a weapon offense. For certain offenses removal can be avoided by a governor's pardon.

The governor's decision was based on, among other things, the "unusual and outstanding equities" of this case.

Shay moaned. "You have got to be kidding me! What kind of justice is that? I wish she *had* been deported."

Don nodded. "It seems she has everyone snowed, that's for sure."

"Maybe she has been rehabilitated, like the article says," Greg said hopefully.

Liza studied the article. "When was this? There's no date."

"There isn't?" Don took the paper from her hands. "Must've gotten lost when it was faxed. I asked the librarian for info from the past month so it's no older than that."

Shay studied Liza. "Do you think she's here, El?"

Liza shrugged. "Honey, I'm just not qualified to make that judgment. I've never met her and can't predict how she'd act. What do you think?"

"I think she won't give up." She lifted a pained expression to Liza, then looked at Don. "What am I going to do?" she whispered.

Liza stood and pulled Shay to her feet. She shook her once, hard, eliciting a gasp from both Don and Greg.

"You are going to pull yourself together, Shay. You're going to fight this bitch with every ounce of your being. I know you're scared, honey, we all are to some extent, but fear won't help you now. I can't believe you would allow this worthless piece of crap to dictate the rest of your life."

"But..." Shay began, staring at Liza with tear-swollen, frightened eyes.

Liza shook her head firmly, her hands still holding Shay's upper arms in a heavy grip. "No buts, Shay. Only you can decide whether you'll be afraid. Don't give in to it. Think of what your parents would want. Do it for them, honey. Be strong for Don. Do it for us, Shay, *us*. I want to build a life with you, but I can't do it if Pepper is in the room with us all the time. Let the fear go, baby. I'm here for you. I'll be here for you, Shay."

For a moment Liza thought she was imagining it, but Shay's back seemed to straighten, her jaw grow more firm. She remained silent for a long while. She looked at Greg. She looked at Don. She looked at Liza. Her temper flared.

"What kind of idiot governor would allow such a psycho to

get out? Now I have to watch my back twenty-four/seven, all because of a stupid loophole and some bleeding heart asshole."

She forcefully shoved Liza's hands aside and stomped around the living room. Greg hastily moved out of her way, and Don watched her with wide eyes.

"I have just about had it with her. She's a heartless...monster. But I don't care. So what if she comes to Alabama? So what if she has my address? It's only a post office box. There's no way she could find me short of following me home from the post office."

"And here, it's wide open, easy to see if someone's following you," Don added.

Shay paused and turned on him vehemently, shaking an index finger toward him. "You're right! That's absolutely right! The roads are huge here, nothing like in DC," she crowed.

"She won't be able to get within a mile of you without you seeing her," Greg chimed in, eager to help.

"She better not let me see her, because I'll run her butt down if I see her first," Shay declared.

Liza stood and pressed both palms toward Shay. "Okay, let's calm down now." She eyed Don angrily. "All of you. Let's talk about this as reasonable adults. I said to be unafraid, *not* crazy."

Shay smiled crookedly, clearly embarrassed. "I just hate the bitch so much, El. What she did to my life is unspeakable. How could she have killed Dr. Frye?"

"I know, honey, and we'll deal with that over time. Just remember, strong baby steps. We'll take things a day at a time and cross the Pepper bridge only when we absolutely have to."

"I still say she better not let me see her following me," Shay said defensively, wiping away new tears brought by thoughts of Rachel Frye.

"Now, Shay, we don't want you in jail..." Don warned. "I agree with Liza. We need to take it easy and speaking of that, I'm turning in, I...I can't deal with any more. It's been a long day for us."

Shay shook her head as if amazed at her own capacity for violence. "I'm sorry, guys; I'm just so pissed."

Don rose and pressed a kiss to Shay's forehead. "No one's blaming you, sweet girl. I didn't know how to tell you, hated to tell you, and Greg and I've been arguing about whether to tell you now or later, just before we leave. It was a tough decision."

"I know, but thank you for coming in person. You didn't have to do that."

"Yes, we did. And you have every right in the world to be upset," he said. "Just don't let fear get the upper hand. You're a lot more powerful than you realize."

Shay nodded and, after both men hugged Liza goodnight, she led the way toward the guest bedroom and helped the men settle in.

"Do you really want to build a life with me?" Shay asked sometime later when she reentered the living room. Liza was sitting in an armchair, gently sloshing an iced amber liquid in her glass. She looked up at Shay, and Shay felt the look all the way to her toes.

"Stay here tonight," Shay whispered. "Can you stay?"

"I'll stay," Liza said, rising and moving to stand with Shay. The electric current between them was all-encompassing. They kissed gently and Shay could taste the bourbon on Liza's breath.

"I'll lock up and be right in," Shay told her. "Get the bed warm."

"No problem there," Liza said with a short laugh.

After Liza quit the room, Shay took a deep breath. Oddly enough, with a house full of people she felt more unafraid than she had in a long time. *My protectors*, she thought as she performed her nightly routine, securing the house. Now if only she could talk all of them into staying here with her forever.

CHAPTER THIRTY-FOUR

The house was empty again after two days of rebonding. Don and Greg, having spent time with Shay *and* accomplishing their unpleasant mission, had flown back north to spend the holiday at the New York home of Don's plump, sweet mother, Adelynn. Shay had met her once at Don's house and fallen head over heels for her. They still e-mailed several times a week.

Liza had gone with her to the airport to see Don and Greg off, but then, as soon as the two returned to Shay's house, had apologetically hurried off, late for a New Life Mission board meeting. She had already called once to check on her and to apologize again for leaving Shay during such a difficult time.

Shay's thoughts meandered to the previous night. Liza had loved her with such gentleness. Though Shay sensed she was filled with avid need, she had restrained it and loved Shay. *Loved* her. With spirit and soul as well as body.

Difficult time.

Shay moved to the bulletin board and studied it. Fear nibbled at the outer corners of her psyche and it was a mighty fight to keep it at bay. Sorrow was prominent as she realized anew the loss of Dr. Frye. She hadn't known, hadn't even been able to go to the funeral. A good thing as Pepper had probably been watching and waiting for her.

Pondering her condition, she realized she felt much stronger than before. Having Liza in her life had changed her somehow. Her total love and acceptance had proven to her that these things were there for her still. During that awful time with Pepper, she had begun to feel alienated from all that was good and whole in life. Losing her parents so quickly after the abuse had further embedded that feeling because the two people who had always loved her that way were abruptly gone. Shay's mindset had become one of isolation, further hemmed in by the ever-present fear of Pepper.

Shay sighed and turned from the bulletin board. She moved to the French doors and imagined she could see the new dog run out back. It was time she rebuilt her life. It was unlikely that she would seek out the prestigious position she'd held in DC and that was okay. She'd been nationally acclaimed as one of the best trainers in the Mid-Atlantic region, an easy title since she *got* dogs and dogs seemed to *get* her. She spoke their language, if one could call it that, a gift she'd possessed since early childhood. The gift was still there and surely she could put it to good use here in the South. She lived simply and had a good financial cushion at the moment, but she would need to go back to work someday. Wanted to go back to work.

Forcing herself to look ahead and not study the surrounding landscape for any sign of intrusion, Shay unlocked the heavy glass doors and the iron cage just outside. She stepped into midday heat bearing the heavy, sultry smells of greenery and nearby water. A blue-black grackle called to her from a tree at the edge of the forested area and she peered into the branches, enjoying the beauty of his dark, iridescent show.

She realized her mind was made up. No longer would she allow Pepper to invade her life. That time was through. She had become a person she no longer recognized: jumpy, irritable, paranoid. She longed for the fun-loving person she'd once been. She knew she could get there again if she grew brave and powerful.

Yet even as this thought passed through her mind, movement to one side caused her heart to lurch and begin racing. She quickly realized it was only the elderly woman who lived next door. The woman stood on her veranda looking out over the landscape. Her white hair was piled high and a dark blue apron covered her housedress. Her features were blurred from this distance, but Shay knew when the woman turned to look her way. Shay could almost pick out her smile as the woman lifted one arm and waved enthusiastically. This was the first time they'd communicated in any way, and Shay's heart thrilled a little at the new connection. She lifted her own arm and waved back.

Brave and powerful. It would take baby steps but she would get there.

CHAPTER THIRTY-FIVE

Liza was down at the far end of the garden when her cell phone rang. She checked the caller ID and was thrilled to see Mindy's name.

"Mindy! Are you okay?" she asked immediately.

"Hey, I'm good. Ro said you were looking for me. Why didn't you just call me?"

"Fear. I was worried it would be bad news about you and Woodpecker. Is everything okay?" Liza braced herself.

Mindy laughed and Liza's heart grew wings. "Much better. I guess I should have called. I'm sorry. We've just been so busy. After Arlie met with you, she came home and we talked all that night and some of the next day. I had no idea she was having the feelings that she was."

"Right, like not being good enough?"

"Umhmm. So now she's seeing a therapist every week over at the clinic to deal with her self-esteem issues. On top of that, we go together for couples counseling over at the MCC in Mobile. It's really helping us deal with some things we didn't even realize were a problem."

Liza breathed a big sigh of relief. "I am so glad."

"So have you seen that little redhead lately?"

"You mean Shay?"

"How many redheads are you seeing?" Mindy laughed.

"Smart-ass. Yes, we're doing better than fine, by the way." She couldn't help the happy note of smugness that crept into her tone.

"Oh, ho! Well, I'm glad Liza. You've been alone way too long as far as I'm concerned."

"I know but that's all changed now. She is special...and wonderful. She was a professional dog trainer. Did you know that?"

"I didn't. How many dogs does she have? I love dogs too."

"Well, that's a long story, best saved for another day. She doesn't have any right now, but I'm going to try and remedy that," Liza stated.

Mindy laughed. "Uh, oh, keep me in the loop on this one."

"No problem. Listen, I want you to let me know if you see any strangers in town. Will you do that?"

Mindy sounded curious. "Sure, will do. Am I looking for anyone in particular?"

"Yep, a woman, probably small. I think all DC people are small."

"Huh?" Mindy really sounded perplexed and Liza laughed.

"Overlook me. I'm delirious in love. Anyway, the woman has blue eyes and short blond hair, probably bleached."

"Okay, I'll be on the lookout, and I'll tell Arlie too."

Liza realized what good friends she had—ones who would take her request at face value without prying. "Thanks, hon, you're okay in my book. Are you coming for Thanksgiving at my house?"

"Nope, can't this year, sweetie. Mom has a new boyfriend and she wants to prove to him what a good cook and homebody she is."

"That should be interesting," Liza said with a short laugh. Mindy's mother was a career real estate tycoon and not known to be warm and fuzzy in any fashion. "Let me know how it goes."

"Will do. Gotta go clean the house before I go to work. Listen, thanks for your help. You really put my baby back on the right path. I can't thank you enough. I'm sorry I didn't call you after."

"Y'all just love and take care of one another, you know? That's all we really have."

"I know, hon. Talk at you later. Next time you hesitate to call me, though, I'll kick your ass. Got it?"

Liza signed off, chuckling to herself. She half-believed Mindy could do it due to Liza's current cotton-wool thoughts. Shay's love was bewitching her. She'd never felt quite so infatuated before or so goofy. She was afraid to go out in public for fear everyone would see just how ridiculous she was acting.

She tried to put thoughts of Shay aside and ponder a decision she needed to finalize. Continuing as business partners with Gina was working out just fine, but Liza worried that by doing so she was compromising her own independence. Financially, it was a very good arrangement as she received full partnership benefits from each quarter's profits. Still, there was a subconscious feeling that she should break free and do something on her own. It was almost as if she was dependent on Gina, even though she certainly did her share of the decision-making.

She paused and looked along the long rows of vegetables that would soon be overripe. She realized suddenly that this wasn't a decision she had to make. At least not alone. Flipping open her cell phone, she pressed a speed dial key.

"Shay, can you come out and play?" she asked as soon as the ringing stopped.

"Play? Not again? Haven't you had enough of me?" Amusement infused Shay's husky voice.

Liza laughed. "Never. So get used to it. Can you come over? I have something I want to show you, maybe get your advice on."

"Sure, be right there. Oh wait, I just realized..." She laughed in disbelief. "I'm not sure I know where you live."

Liza laughed for a long time—so long she could sense Shay

fuming on the other end of the line. She stopped abruptly, gave Shay directions, signed off, then laughed some more, shaking her head in amazement. Talk about insanity. As intimate as they'd been, Shay had yet to meet her family or visit her home. She'd fix that oversight in a hurry.

CHAPTER THIRTY-SIX

"So anyway, Dee is going to check into it and see if he can learn her whereabouts," Shay said as they strolled around to the backyard at Liza's house. "I still *cannot* believe that she was released."

"I can't either. I told Mindy to keep an eye out for strangers too. She said she would."

"Good. We should probably....whoa!" She broke off abruptly as Liza's garden came into view. "Oh, my gosh, El. What have you done?"

Liza frowned and hastened to defend her work. "Well, I was alone then and had to do something with my time. Besides this is what I do, you know?"

Shay turned bright eyes upon Liza. "I do know, and this is wonderful! So this is what you were talking about the other day."

Liza smiled tremulously. "You mean it's okay? You like it?"

"Oh, honey, this is so much more than okay. How do you get everything so green? And I don't see a single weed. How do you do that? You have people working it, of course," she told herself.

Liza shook her head in the negative. "Nope, do it all myself. Or used to. I've been a little distracted lately." She pulled Shay into her embrace and they shared a yielding kiss.

"This is why I wanted you to come over. I have some major decisions to make and would like your input." She reluctantly moved back. "I'm trying to decide whether to break my partnership with Meadows, to maybe go out on my own."

"Ah." Shay thought a long beat. "Have you made the pro and con list? That always helps me."

"The what?"

"The list. The positives and negatives of making the change or staying the same."

"Hmm, hadn't thought of that. I mean, I've thought a lot about the issue but haven't put anything concrete on paper."

Shay studied Liza with her head tilted to one side. "Is there a problem staying with Meadows?"

The other woman shrugged. "No, not really. I don't usually have to deal with Gina, not that I have a real problem with her. And the money is great because the business is huge and does so well."

"And you can easily support your philanthropy jones," Shay added.

Liza looked at her and burst into laughter. "My philanthropy jones? Omigosh, you are so cute!"

Shay grinned. "Well, it's true. The resources there allow you to help a lot of people."

Liza realized she hadn't thought of that aspect. "You know, you're right. It would be much harder to do that on my own."

"These are all things you need to think about when making a decision like this. How would the change impact your life for good or for bad?" She leaned and touched a plump green bean. "Can I eat this?"

"Help yourself, sweetheart," Liza answered absently, her mind digesting Shay's common sense observations.

"Man, that's good," Shay said savoring the bite of raw green bean. "The soil here must be incredible."

"Well, I've prepared it, of course, but you're right, the base is very good here. Close to the water table. Come with me, I want to show you something else."

"Omigosh, are those strawberries?" Shay asked, veering toward the papaya trees.

Liza sighed and rolled her eyes in mock disgust. "Help yourself," she said.

Watching Shay forage gave Liza an intense feeling of pleasure.

"I simply cannot believe you are growing all this back here," Shay said, offering a berry to Liza.

Liza popped the berry into her mouth, then took Shay's hand and led her through the length of the garden and into the wilderness beyond. Shay was surprised to find herself surrounded by bright Christmas trees bearing large yellow ornaments. When a delicious citrus scent penetrated, she realized she was actually surrounded by a grove of heavily laden grapefruit trees, something she'd never seen before. With the trees planted in close rows, she could easily have become lost amidst the mass of them.

"Did you plant these?" she asked, fluttering her fingers through the rough greenery.

"Oh no, they've been here about thirty years. The people who owned this place, before my dad and mom bought it back in the late seventies, had a whole grove. Lots have died back because no one has taken care of them. Most, like these here, are doing well, though, feeding the birds and the possums—and me—each year."

Liza noticed Shay's hungry look and quickly plucked a mottled green fruit from the tree and handed it to her. "Here, try one. This is a ruby, so it is way sweet. Do you like grapefruit?"

Shay answered by fixing Liza's eyes in a hungry gaze and biting into the peel of the fruit, pulling it from the pulp with her teeth. The action made Liza melt in all the right places. Her eyes darkened with desire.

"My, my," she whispered. "I guess you do."

Liza pulled Shay close and kissed her long and hard, the bitter tang of the grapefruit peel welcome on her lips. Shay returned the kiss, entwining her hands, one holding the grapefruit, behind Liza's head. Her hips pressed ardently into the taller woman and Liza felt her knees weaken. It was about time she found a woman with the exact perfect chemistry and a desire that matched her own. Breaking the kiss, she hung her head, mentally thanking the universe for sending her such perfection.

She lifted her gaze and noted how secluded they were, totally hidden by the trees. Luckily, the trees hadn't been trimmed so the lower branches remained to shield the two women further. Her father never came down to this part of the yard and her brother was at work. Perfect.

Giving in to her desire, she kissed Shay again, then lifted her shirt, delighted to find nothing beneath the soft cotton. She teased the hardening breast tips with her mouth until Shay's heartbeat and breathing increased. Impatiently, Liza unsnapped Shay's jeans and pulled open the zipper. She moved to one side and lowered their bodies gently to a cleared area below one of the trees. Holding Shay close with her left arm as a cushion beneath her, Liza allowed her free hand to tease, roaming Shay's neck, body and breasts as she pressed kisses upon her. Sometime later, she pushed her hand down inside Shay's jeans and found the sweetness there. Their lips met and held, tongues dancing sensuously as Liza's hand rhythmically, yet slowly, taking her time, moved against the softness, pushing Shay over the edge. After some time, her uncontrolled wail sounded in Liza's mouth, and Liza felt empathic sensations race along her thighs and belly. Pulling her hand free, she cradled Shay in her arms, the rabble-rouser grapefruit still held snugly between their bodies.

"Lord, what you do to me," Shay muttered sometime later, her gaze fuzzy. She stood with Liza's help and waited, quietly obedient and nibbling the grapefruit, as Liza refastened the jeans she'd so recently opened, straightened Shay's shirt and brushed debris from her clothing and hair. Shay's cheeks were pink and her embarrassment further endeared her to Liza.

"There, all better," Liza said, patting Shay's clothing. "No one's the wiser."

Shay smiled mischievously. "I guess I'll have to owe you one," she teased.

"Something to look forward to," Liza added, her voice growing husky. "Let's make it soon, okay?"

Shay laughed at Liza's drawn features. "Soon, baby," she assured her.

"You know, this is really good," Shay said as they slowly walked along the trees. "Have you thought about growing these, as a business?"

"Actually," Liza mused thoughtfully. "I could. Growing them could be a side industry, especially if I opened my own business. I see your point though. Giving up Meadows would be silly at this point in my life. I can't imagine anything making me more money than I make there, and you're right about the charity work—my philanthropy jones, as you call it." Her lips curved with amusement as she said the term. "Besides, competing with Meadows might not be in my best interest."

Shay handed Liza a section of fruit as they walked back toward the garden. "You know..." Shay mused. "What if you had a Meadows South? As a part of the original Meadows. Like a new branch, a new division."

Liza stopped walking and stilled. She hadn't thought of that. "That's a great idea. I could even use the Meadows resources, giving the part-time workers something to do when they're idle up there. We're warmer than they are. You're a genius, Shay!"

Shay grinned proudly, clearly pleased that she had helped Liza with a major decision. She lifted her face for one more kiss.

Inside the house, Shay took in the worn, comfortable surroundings of the large farmhouse and realized they fit Liza exactly. She wasn't one to put on airs and, as long as items remained functional, Shay knew Liza, with her reduce/reuse/recycle mentality, would utilize them as long as possible.

A man strongly resembling Liza, to whom Shay was soon introduced, eyed her with friendly curiosity as he took her hand.

"So you're the young lady my Liza's been hanging out

with," Tom Hughes said jovially. "It's good to finally meet you."

"My dad's a nurse over at Fairhope General," Liza said.

Shay's eyes widened. "Oh, no way! My father was a nurse like forever until he finally took an administrative position."

Tom tilted his head to one side. "Really. Which hospital? I may have met him at a seminar."

"GWU. He also worked in administration in the medical school. He was a lot older than you. His name was Thaddeus Raynor."

"Hmm, tall thin man? Balding?"

Shay's smile broadened. "Yes! How weird is that?"

Liza looked at Shay, then at her father. "You don't mean to tell me you knew Shay's dad?"

Her father nodded. "Yep, not well but I met him on several occasions. I remember a great presentation he gave at a session in Florida several years ago. It was on decreasing staff load by increasing volunteer possibilities in communities."

"That was a topic dear to his heart," Shay said, eyes growing fond. "So what is your specialty?"

"I get to work in neonatal. With the babies. I'm afraid that I'll be following in your father's footsteps, however. If the powers that be have their way, I'll be driving a desk for a while."

"Dad's been fighting skin cancer," Liza explained, "and the treatments have left him a little weak. They're just taking him off the floor temporarily until he gets all his strength back. Shouldn't be long but he'll be going back to a desk job after the holidays."

Shay eyed him closely. "Well, you look well for a man who's been sick. I hope your recovery is swift."

Liza took Shay's hand and pulled her toward the kitchen. "Gotta go, Pop. We're making the menu for tomorrow."

Shay shrugged helplessly as she was tugged away. "Nice meeting you, Mr. Hughes."

"Tom, call me Tom," he called after them, "and make sure y'all make some of that sweet potato casserole, with the marshmallows on top."

CHAPTER THIRTY-SEVEN

Later, at the large, fluorescently lit grocery store in Fairhope, Shay playfully climbed onto the front rail of Liza's metal grocery cart and chattered nonstop as she and Liza searched for Thanksgiving fixings. The basket already held a huge turkey, a ham, a large bag of fresh cranberries, salted butter and assorted miscellaneous items, and the two of them were arguing about whether to use prepackaged stuffing or make their own from fresh bread crumbs as they traveled at a good clip down the milk aisle. As they rounded a corner, their cart was broadsided by another, creating a huge clang. Shay went tumbling off the cart, sprawling onto the vinyl floor. Terrified, Liza stood frozen, mouth agape. To add to her astonishment, she saw that Kim was pushing the other cart with Rosemary trailing behind. They seemed to be as much in shock as she was, but all three women quickly came to their senses and converged on Shay to help her regain her feet.

Liza pressed and tested all Shay's long bones with frantic hands. "Oh, Shay, are you okay? I am so sorry. I was going way too fast."

"And I wasn't even looking," Kim said quickly. "Please tell us you're okay."

Shay's head was bowed, her unbound red hair stretched taut across her face where it was caught in the collar of her blouse. Liza moved to embrace her so she could comfort her more completely. "Please don't cry. Where are you hurt? Ro, call an ambulance."

Rosemary moved closer and took each of Shay's arms in turn to check for injury as Liza pushed the hair back from Shay's face. It was then that they realized the woman's shoulders were shaking from silent laughter, not injury. Tears were spilling but with amusement, not pain. Liza breathed a huge sigh of relief as Shay's laughter finally sounded.

"Did you guys see that?" Shay crowed. "If I'd had wings, I could have flown."

Rosemary laughed, relieved. "I bet you slid twenty feet," she offered.

Kim took a deep breath. "Are you sure nothing's hurt, sprained, broken?"

Liza was still examining Shay, turning her around and holding her so she could brush dust from her jeans, oblivious to the woman's struggles for freedom.

"Okay, El, okay! Leggo. I'm fine, really," she said as she extricated herself.

"Do you think we should take her over to the hospital and let them have a look at her?" Liza asked Rosemary, her voice earnest and worried.

"Oh no, I'm hungry and you promised me lunch," Shay replied before Rosemary could respond.

"But hon, what if..." Liza began.

"Hungry," Shay interjected firmly.

"But..."

"Hungry."

Rosemary laughed at Shay's determination. "Well, lunch it is. Ya' ll want to go over next door to the deli and have subs? They're really good there."

"Yes, yes," Shay said excitedly.

Kim was watching Shay, marveling at how changed she seemed to be. "Okay, let's finish up and meet up front in, say," she looked at her watch, "fifteen minutes?"

Once they were settled in the restaurant with cold iced teas before each of them, Kim looked at Shay. "Well, something sure has you happy these days," she said bluntly.

"Kim! Behave," Rosemary hissed. "Excuse her, Shay, she's a Yankee and has no home training."

"I'm just saying she's not looking over her shoulder all the time like she used to. That's all."

Liza laughed and mimed suggestively, "Well, it's having me in her life, of course. That's probably what has perked her up."

Shay looked at Liza with a pained expression, then laughed. She turned to Kim. "I'm glad you noticed. That means it's working."

Liza shifted so she could see Shay more clearly. "Working? What's working?"

Shay sipped iced tea through a straw and calmly regarded her lover. "My decision."

Kim exploded after a lengthy silence. "Shay, I'm going to wring your neck if you don't tell us what the devil you're talking about."

Shay appeared chastened. "I'm sorry, I'm not really trying to be coy."

"Yes, you are," teased Rosemary. "Just admit it."

"It's because she knows how cute she is doing it," offered Liza.

Kim pointedly cleared her throat, effectively ending the foolishness.

Shay took a deep breath and began to tell the story of her relationship with Pepper at length, pausing only while the sandwiches were delivered.

"Anyway, the therapy with poor Dr. Frye was really helpful, but after Dee told me the other night that Pepper had been released, I felt as though something snapped. All the next day, even while Dee and Greg were leaving, I kept hearing Dr. Frye's words. Like she was a ghost talking in my ear. She always said it was up to me whether or not I lived a fearful life. That I could always choose whether to be afraid."

"Well," Kim began, then paused to chew and swallow, "I agree. But don't negate visceral fear, that gut-level fear that we all have that keeps us safe."

Shay waved one hand. "I don't even have to think about that, just trust my body to do what is necessary. When Liza shook me the other night..." She saw their expressions and grinned. "Yes, she did, right there in front of Dee and Greg. She was so butch."

Rosemary looked at Liza, eyes wide. She'd never known her friend to be violent in any way. Liza stared calmly in return.

"Anyway, when she shook me, she said that the two of us would never fully be a couple with Pepper always in the room between us. I realized that was true." She took Liza's hand and squeezed it.

"That next morning I woke happier than I had been in years. Loving Liza is more important than the worst-case scenarios that I'd been living my daily life by."

"So, what? You're not afraid at all anymore?" Kim frowned as she added more mustard to her sandwich.

Shay hastened to assure her differently. "No, I am, I mean, of course. Pepper could be here in town trying to find me. I know I still need to be extremely careful. I gotta tell you though, there were a lot of days I was suicidal because of my fear. It's not fair to make someone, anyone, deal with that."

She paused to gaze lovingly at Liza and squeeze her hand one more time before letting go and lifting her sandwich.

Rosemary spoke up, adding sensibly. "It's not fair to you either. You deserve more, a chance at a good life."

"Especially after what she did to you," Kim finished.

Chewing, Shay nodded in agreement. "I do. I will. Finding Liza has been a gift. She even tolerates my Irish temper without flinching too much."

Rosemary laughed. "I've known her twenty years and have yet to see her really lose her cool. And there's been lots of opportunities, let me tell you. She's tolerated a lot more than I ever could."

"I did get a little testy the day Shay and I met, though," Liza replied. "She was a total, well, you know." She winked and eyed Shay merrily.

Shay lifted her eyebrows but didn't respond, too busy eating to comment.

Kim balled up her napkin and sat back, hands folded on her stomach. "So what does Pepper look like? We'll help watch out for her and will let you know right away if we see her."

Liza answered for Shay. "She's small, Shay says, like her. She has a super short haircut, like a buzz cut, that she bleaches blond, and she has really bright blue eyes. Kind of ballsy too, from the picture I saw of her."

"She has an accent, British. And a nice smile when she wants to and can charm the pants right off you," added Shay around a mouthful. "I've seen her smooth talk lots of women and she always gets her way."

"Sounds like a winner," Rosemary commented dryly. "I can't believe you got messed up with her."

Shay shrugged. "Biggest regret of my life."

After another thirty minutes of chatting, the four women reluctantly rose to leave. Liza reacted with alarm when Shay cried out and clutched her back. "Oh, no. See? I told you we should have had you checked out."

Shay laid one hand on Liza's shoulder and frowned. "Can't a girl be sore, El? You just threw me twenty feet across a tile floor and you expect me to..."

"What do you mean, I threw you! I would never..." Liza paused when she saw Shay's teasing smile. "That's it. You're going straight to my house and right to bed."

Rosemary and Kim stood to one side, watching the two with some amusement.

"That's what you think," Shay argued. "We have a powerful lot of cooking to do."

"We? I don't think so, you're going to rest. Maybe you can offer advice but that's it. I don't want you so much as lifting a can of peas."

Shay's face was growing red and Kim quickly interrupted. "So, Liza, what time is dinner?"

"We'll eat early enough so you can make it back in time to serve at the mission," she assured her. "Come about one."

"Is everyone coming this year?" Ro asked.

"Mindy and Woodpecker can't, but *Mémé* is coming and Steve's family so it'll be a full house."

Ro studied Shay. "Girl, you have no idea what you're in for. Thanksgiving at the Hughes house is a circus."

"And a ton of fun," Kim added. "We wouldn't miss it for the world."

"Omigosh," Liza cried suddenly. "I forgot to call *Mémé*. I need to pick her up on the way home."

Laughing Ro and Kim passed out farewell hugs and crawled into their small hybrid car. They beeped once gaily as they pulled out of the parking lot.

"Such cool women," Shay commented as Liza dug her cell phone out of her jeans pocket.

"That they are," Liza agreed as she flipped open the phone. "Let me call *Mémé* and we'll be on our way."

CHAPTER THIRTY-EIGHT

After stopping by Shay's house so they could pick up an overnight bag, including the bottle of over-the-counter pain reliever that Liza knew Shay would need after her fall, Liza pulled up in front of the huge mansion at Placide's Place. The large drive formed a sweeping curve just south of Shay's house. Shay realized suddenly that the woman on the veranda was Liza's grandmother.

"Duh," she said aloud.

Liza looked at her in alarm. "Are you okay?" Her face screwed into a moue of sympathy. "Hurting?"

"I am so stupid. I just realized that this is where your grandmother lives. I can't believe I didn't put two and two together, especially after you knew my property so well. You even said she lived close to me."

Liza laughed and came around to help Shay from the truck. "Well, it's not like you've had anything else to think about."

Shay agreed and followed Liza up the wide front steps and into a cool wood-paneled foyer. "Where you at, *Mémé?*" she called gently.

Shay studied the elegant, historic home as she followed Liza slowly through the narrow rooms. Spotlessly clean and pleasingly furnished, the home, which could easily have been heavy and daunting, was comfortable and welcoming. They stepped into a large, rustic kitchen, then passed through a long hallway that opened into a huge solarium filled with fragrant greenery; some, by their thick, twisted branches, appeared old and well established. Even the wooden-framed panes of glass were ancient, bearing hand warping and numerous imperfections.

"She must be upstairs getting ready," Liza mused. Within seconds, they had passed through several maze-like rooms and mounted a large, polished wood staircase. Liza held Shay's elbow, helping her along.

"Are you sure this is okay?" Shay whispered. "She won't get mad at us for coming in this way, will she?"

Liza laughed at Shay's worry. "You wait. You'll meet her soon, and then you tell me."

At the top of the staircase, Shay spied a second stairway that obviously led to the top veranda. She paused and Liza turned to her.

"You want to go up there?" Liza offered. "It's quite a view."

Shay nodded and Liza took her arm. Moments later, they were standing outside a heavy metal-bound pine door and breathing in a freshened breeze and a breathtaking vista.

"Oh, my heavens," Shay whispered.

Liza grinned like a kid. "Awesome, isn't it? I used to spend a lot of time up here."

"This is incredible. I bet you can see all the way to Florida from here."

Liza agreed. "I think so. Really. And look over here. You can see your place."

Shay moved to the north side. Her house looked like a quaint little cottage from this height. Shay took a moment to judge the property spatially. "Hey, El, what do you think about putting a dog lot right there?"

She pointed to a mostly cleared expanse just outside and downhill from the back stoop.

Liza stepped closer. "You mean along that tree line? To train?"

"And board. Wouldn't it be cool to run a kennel to board dogs while people travel? You could offer grooming and training services too."

Liza watched Shay, her eyes fond. "*You* could, you mean. I think that would be a great idea, Shay."

Shay lifted her eyes to Liza and her heart ached from the love she saw there. The pride too. She felt so good in that moment, so complete. She lifted her lips to Liza's in a gentle kiss.

"Thank you for believing in me," she whispered against Liza's lips.

"Mmm," Liza pulled her into a gentle embrace. No passion this time, just a loving comfort. Both women sighed with pleasure.

"Okay," Shay said, pulling away. "Decision made. Now, we need to get the groceries home before they spoil in this heat."

"Party pooper," Liza teased.

They found *Mémé* in her bedroom by following the pervasive fragrance of Heavensent perfume. Entering the huge salon, Shay felt a pang of loss for all the homes that no longer had luxurious sitting rooms attached to their master bedrooms. She touched one of the buff silk Queen Anne chairs and noted the matching footstool. How lovely to sit here in the evenings watching the sunset through the huge west-facing bay window.

"Wow, someone sure smells good," Liza said, approaching the open bathroom door.

A stream of rapid French, spoken like a true native, emerged through the open door.

"English, *Mémé*. English. Come out here, I want you to meet Shay, your next-door neighbor."

Moments later, a regal woman emerged. Dressed in a Chanel-styled pantsuit with long white hair braided intricately around her skull, she was the epitome of the classic beauty, albeit one in the evening of her life. She eyed Shay with keen eyes, then broke into a wide smile. She rushed toward Shay and took her hand between her own parchment palms. "So good to meet you finally. I waved to you, yes? I saw the flame hair." One hand moved to indicate her own white tresses as if to help Shay understand. "Yes, I saw you too. I waved." Shay blushed, realizing how stupid her remark sounded. She was positively taken aback by the lovely, self-assured woman.

"Shay, this is my grandmother, Rosaries Hinto. *Mémé*, Shay Raynor," Liza said, making the formal introduction. She lifted the small case and shawl resting on the curved sofa. "Is this everything, *Mémé*?"

Rosaries nodded, "*Oui*." She was still studying Shay, as if knowing she had stolen Liza's heart. She spoke slowly, her voice gentle. "You call me Rose or *Mémé*. We shall be great friends."

CHAPTER THIRTY-NINE

Tom and Rich were both at home when they arrived and helped unload the groceries while Liza focused on helping *Mémé* and a very sore Shay from the cab of the truck. The drive in had been interesting. *Mémé*, perched between the two of them, had asked Shay probing questions about her life and family during the entire drive to Bon Secour. The elderly woman was an expert at genteelly ferreting out information, and Liza now knew more about Shay's life than before. Oddly enough, Shay didn't appear to feel as though her privacy had been invaded. The Canadian woman was a master and had even gently pried out the story of Pepper's abuse.

Once inside, Liza forced Shay and *Mémé* into chairs at the kitchen table, then toted their overnight bags upstairs, placing *Mémé*'s bag into Rich's bedroom and Shay's bag into hers. She took time for one more quick glance around her bedroom. Though still bearing worn relics of her childhood, it was presentable.

As soon as Liza was out of the room, Rosaries stood and clicked open her vinyl handbag. She removed a large cloth apron which she pulled over her head and tied in back.

"Ridiculous to sit," she muttered to herself as she moved to the sink and unpacked the nearest cloth grocery bag.

Shay watched in amazement as Rosaries expertly moved through the kitchen. She knew where everything was located and soon had placed a large pot of salted water next to the sink and was snipping open the protective wrapping on the enormous turkey. Shay rose and began unpacking bags as well, placing the contents onto the counter and folding the empties into a neat pile.

Rich entered with another load and eyed Shay doubtfully. Shay smiled and took the bags from him.

"Hi, Rich, good to see you again," she said cheerfully. "You remember me, don't you? Shay, from CM's place?"

Rich blushed and nodded briefly at her before darting out the back door.

Rosaries studied the flapping door. "My grandson, the wit," she said apologetically.

Shay laughed as she continued to place grocery items on the counter.

"Whoa, you two!" Liza cried as she entered the kitchen. "I thought I told you both to sit still."

"Since when do I take the orders from you?" Rosaries retorted as she washed the turkey in the sink.

"Yeah," Shay agreed.

Tom entered and placed two more bags on the table. He paused and looked at his wife's mother. "How have you been, Rose?"

Rosaries paused in her work, dried her hands and moved to hug her son-in-law. She reared back and studied his face. "We are well, *non*?"

Tom, speechless, just nodded and pulled her into another lengthy embrace.

Breaking the moment, Liza cleared her throat. "Pop, you

know I'm never going to learn to cook if *Mémé* keeps doing it. Every time I say to her 'just watch me to make sure I'm doing it right' and look what she does."

"Liza, you're an intelligent woman," Tom said, smiling. "Seems like you'd understand how it works by now. Rosaries will no more sit idle than that bayou out there will dry up next week."

"Fine!" Liza said petulantly. "I guess I'll just have to learn by osmosis." She began earnestly dividing canned goods as the others laughed.

Tom wandered into the relative safety of the living room, and Shay jumped in to help with the preparations. Rosaries and Liza started talking then, about Liza's mother, Rosaries' daughter, Sienna. Thanksgiving had been the time she enjoyed most because she loved her big family after being an only child. This could have resulted in a maudlin discussion, but Shay was amazed to see it veer off into a celebration of Sienna's life and all the positives she'd brought to the family. Obviously, the upbeat spirit of this woman had made a memorable mark on all their lives.

The sheer quantity of food amazed Shay as well. It would seem that the Hughes family knew how to eat well. That or the guest list had to be huge. Liza and Rosaries worked well together as they effortlessly produced the immense feast. They prepared the turkey with a coating of herbed butter, stuffing it with chopped celery, onion, and herbs from the garden, and then Liza placed it into the bottom of a two-oven set-up built into one wall of the kitchen. A ham, dotted with cloves, butter and brown sugar went into the top oven. That done, the duo worked as a team to unroll store-bought pastry into six pie pans and mix the fillings. Shay saw a large bowl of pecans become a gooey, caramelized concoction. Green apples, dark, burgundy cherries and canned pumpkin were prepared and doctored to become something magical under Rosaries' firm guidance.

Feeling like a third wheel, Shay focused on cleanup duties, steadfastly claiming the territory around the sink to wash and dry necessary pans, implements and platters for reuse. One thing her mother had taught her well was how to make sweet tea and she made pitcher after pitcher of it whenever she had a moment free from dishes.

Several hours later, with prepackaged items divided into organized groupings on the counter for tomorrow's preparation, all that was left was to let the meat finish cooking so the pies could bake.

The three women made themselves glasses of sweet iced tea, Rosaries officially removed her apron, and they retired to the patio just outside the back door. They took seats at the cast-iron table and cooled themselves with the frosty tea and a subtle late afternoon breeze. The sound of the television, watched by Tom and Rich, floated out to them but it was a pleasant background murmur, not intrusive at all.

Shay studied the attractive, highly functional courtyard that the Hughes family had created outside the kitchen door. Though situated next to the door so groceries could be easily unloaded from vehicles, the gravel drive gave way to soapstone flagstones as the drive passed the house. The patio covered a thirty- or forty-foot circular area that stretched from the side of the house proper across to the scrubby, forested area, bordering the bayou on the far side and the clearing of the Hughes' house lot. Surrounded by low Mexican palms and other luxurious greenery Shay could never hope to identify, the patio bore several tables and a half dozen redwood benches set into mulched rows along the house wall. Beyond the patio, toward the back was the glorious product of Liza's green thumb.

Rosaries studied Liza's garden as it stretched out before them. "I don't know how this is," she said gently. "You have the gift, *certainment*."

Liza nodded and took Shay's hand, just to connect. "Some people cook. Some people talk to dogs. Some people grow. Now I just need to get some people to harvest. I'm trying to wrap my head around getting the Meadows workers down here at just the right times."

"Oh, because the crops ripen at different times," Shay nodded her understanding.

"Yep." Liza nodded in return and lifted her tea. "It's not cost effective for them to bring the trucks here so many times and leave them while the workers pick. We use those trucks every day for pickups and deliveries. I need to talk possibilities over with Gina, but I guess I'll wait until after the holidays."

"But will the plants wait?" Rosaries commented archly.

Liza shrugged. "Some are ready now but not much I can do about it."

Shay scratched her chin. "Liza, I was just thinking...what if you got up with Ro and maybe used some of the mission people to pick? I mean, they are homeless and not working..."

If someone had hit Liza in the back of the head with a shovel, her expression couldn't have been more shocked than by Shay's idea. She could not believe the notion had never occurred to her in all her agony over getting the crops handled properly. Her mind whirled with new possibilities.

Rosaries watched the two of them. She chuckled and sighed. "Liza, *mon très cher*, in this one you have found a...a *camarade d'âmie*."

Liza laughed and nodded her agreement, yet remained distracted as her attention still circled around preliminary plans for Meadows South. A pleasant silence fell.

Shay fumed, however, growing ever more petulant. "Well," she said finally, after many minutes had passed. "What does it mean?"

Liza shook herself from reverie and laughed. She pulled Shay's hand closer. "She says we're soul mates. Something we already knew."

CHAPTER FORTY

"Okay, here's the deal. After you feed and water in the afternoon, take her up to the house and tie her to the porch railing. Do you have the bow? Be sure and put it on the back of the new collar so she can't chew it. Umhmm, it's in the drawer under the cat kennels, on the right."

Liza sat curled into a fetal position in one of the kitchen chairs, a hot cup of coffee cradled in her free hand. Her other hand held her cell. Shay, she hoped, was still asleep in Liza's bedroom, snuggled next to the pillow Liza had pressed to her as she left the bed. It was only six o'clock, but Liza knew this would be the best time to talk with Chris, who was at the shelter caring for the animals. It had been several years since Carol and Paul had both been able to take the morning shift off on a holiday and Liza was ever grateful to Christine for that.

She gave directions to Shay's house and quickly signed off before someone came into the kitchen and caught her. It was just in time too, for *Mémé* appeared in the doorway. "*Bonjour*, Liza. You are early this day."

Liza studied her grandmother, who was already dressed for the day in casual slacks, a bright blue blouse and pearls at ears and neck. She even wore low heels. Liza felt way under dressed in her pajama shorts and T-shirt. "Yep, thought I'd get an early start on the cooking."

"How did the bird do the night?" Rosaries poured a cup of coffee and then fetched milk from the refrigerator. She drank her coffee as Chloe did, with lots of milk and sugar.

Liza uncurled herself and moved over to the large industrial cooler situated by the refrigerator. Lifting the top a fraction, she slid her hand inside. "Still cold. Works every year, especially after we got those larger ice blocks."

"My Sienna was no fool," Rosaries stated as she seated herself at the table.

"I wish she could have met Shay," Liza said, resuming her seat. "Do you think she would have liked her?"

"*Oui, certainment.* My Sienna think like me, what's not to like? Beautiful, sweet girl. If you happy, Sienna will be good with it."

Hearing this meant a lot to Liza. No one knew Sienna as well as her own mother. An only child, Sienna and her mother had been best friends.

Liza rose, cup in hand, and briefly embraced her grandmother with one arm. "Well, I'll go shower and see how that beautiful, sweet girl feels this morning. We need to start getting the rest together because the hungry brood'll be here soon."

"*Bon*," Rosaries agreed as she stood and buried her head in the crowded fridge seeking breakfast fixings.

Upstairs, Shay slept on, exactly where Liza had left her. She looked adorable, her body curved into a sprawling letter C around Liza's pillow. Liza watched her for some time, noting how the deep copper-rust of her hair seemed so brilliant against the white of the bed linens. Having Shay in her bedroom thrilled Liza for some odd reason. It was as if having her in this central point of Liza's private life somehow magically pulled Shay into a deeper level of importance. Liza felt draped in grateful revelry. They were so fortunate to have found one another. Maybe all the bad that had happened to Shay was for this reason, to bring her to this place of rightness. Liza knew one thing for certain. She'd spend the rest of her life making sure that no one ever hurt Shay again.

Liza sighed and set her coffee to one side. She slid into the bed and pulled Shay to her, the pillow between them.

"I wondered how long you were going to stand there watching me," Shay murmured. "Make any grand decisions?"

Liza drew back in surprise. "I thought you were still asleep!"

Shay rolled onto her back, throwing her left arm wide. She groaned loudly. "I was until some lead foot came in bearing the wonderful scent of coffee."

"Would you like some?"

Shay opened one eye and peeped at Liza. "Of yours?"

"Of course, or you can have your own..." She noticed Shay's randy glance and stilled. "Oh no you don't, Rich's room is right next to this one."

"Hmm, guess you're right. Your grandmother would be embarrassed by the sounds we'd make." She sighed in frustration.

"Actually, *Mémé is* the kitchen..." She reconsidered. "Nope, too much to do. Bad woman, trying to lead me down the path of debauchery."

Shay laughed and tried to rise but fell back. "Ouch! That tumble I took did a number on me."

Liza was immediately remorseful. "Poor baby, let's get you into a hot shower."

"Alone?" Shay stood carefully and stretched carefully.

"Well, I *do* have my own bathroom," Liza said, lifting her eyebrows a la Groucho Marx.

Shay grinned and took Liza's hand, pulling her into the bathroom and closing the door firmly behind them.

Shay's hands slid under Liza's shirt and gently stroked her back as Liza leaned to adjust the water flow and temperature. Liza closed her eyes, relishing the caress. She turned and pulled Shay close. Their kiss lasted an eternity. Liza's tongue pushed deep into Shay and Shay felt her knees weaken from the erotic onslaught.

Within moments, they were undressed and the steamy scent of their passion surrounded them. Liza, eyes dark and demanding, pulled Shay into the shower. They languidly soaped each other's bodies, eyes full of promise and sharing deep, sporadic kisses that left them dizzy and wanting more. Shay pressed her soapy hand between Liza's legs as her tongue teased nipples that were erect and insistent. Liza watched the action greedily as her own hand slid easily into Shay. Her thumb strummed Shay's clit gently. Gasps of delight surrounded them as they merged into one being, erotically charged and eventually, quietly, sated.

CHAPTER FORTY-ONE

Shay, as an only child to older parents, was used to family gatherings that were quiet, subdued affairs. Watching Liza's youthful, energetic family interact was like watching a hilarious sitcom married to a soap opera.

Everyone seemed happy to gather except for Liza's older brother, Steve. He was a handsome man, with dark, snapping eyes and sleek black hair, but that was where the goodness ended. He seemed full of superior attitude and unable to relax among the peons of his family. He was dressed in a dark suit and tie. One could tell this was his usual daily garb and that the power suit was what he felt most comfortable wearing. He appeared glad to see his grandmother and father, but Shay could tell there was no love lost between Steve and Liza.

Mary, his wife, was blond, plump and wore a weary air as though it were a protective robe. Their son, Mason, dark like his father, was a typical preteen attached to ear buds and an electronic game. Their daughter, Stevie, who was only six, was a delight and, Shay could tell, held a special place in Liza's heart. The child had long blond hair, tied back in a thick ponytail, and huge blue eyes. Her thumb had a sneaky way of finding her mouth quite often and her favorite pastime was lap sitting. Shay adored her immediately.

Liza's sister, Chloe, was a knockout; Shay envied her. How could anyone look that well pulled together so effortlessly? Wearing perfectly fitted, low-slung jeans and a form-fitting tank top, she could have been a magazine model come to life. She was with an equally beautiful man named Scott who worked with her at a law firm.

Shay had a hard time pulling her eyes away from Chloe and several times caught Liza watching her with amusement as they worked with Rosaries to prepare the last of the feast. The family members and guests, for some reason, as they arrived and entered through the kitchen door, invariably huddled around the kitchen table to catch up. This slowed preparations considerably as introductions were made and attention was distracted from the tasks at hand. Eventually, however, everything was prepared or reheated and placed along the countertops in the kitchen. Rosaries fetched Tom from the man huddle in the living room, and he delivered a brief blessing.

"I only wish our dear Sienna could be here to enjoy this meal with those she loved the most," he said after the amens had sounded.

"She is here, Papa," Stevie said quickly. "Can't you feel her?" She popped her thumb back into her mouth as Rosaries pulled her close. Tom cleared his throat, as if trying to choke back sudden tears.

"Well, let's eat," Steve said as he made his way to the stack of plates.

Chatter took over then as everyone filled his or her plate and searched for a good place to sit.

The Hughes family ate everywhere, a practice very different from Shay's family who ate at the dining table only. Shay found she rather liked the informality of it. She and Liza sat with Ro and Kim at the table outside by the garden. Stevie had brought her plate along as well and had taken residence in Liza's lap as she ate. Liza seemed to enjoy the contact even though the squirming girl made it more difficult to eat her meal. Shay realized anew that the woman she loved *was* as easygoing as everyone said. If she were ever to have a child, this would be the type of person she would want as the other mother. Fantasies of a future family with Liza warmed her into silence.

"They're cranberries, Stevie. Try them, they're good," Liza said.

Stevie was not convinced, making a face and spitting the red berries back onto her plate as Ro and Kim laughed.

"That's pretty rude, rugrat," Liza said.

Her gaze found Shay and lingered lovingly. "Are you okay?"

Shay smiled and cocked her head to one side. "Absolutely," she replied. "Aren't you going to tell them about the garden?"

Ro speared another forkful of roasted potato. "It's really beautiful out here, Liza. You have such a green thumb. I don't know how you do it."

"It's backbreaking labor," added Kim. "I'd rather make twenty beds than weed just one of those rows."

Liza shrugged. "I love it, the quiet, the heat on my back, the smell of the earth."

"Ewww," Stevie offered, wrinkling her sun-pinkened nose. "There's germs and bugs in the dirt, Mama says."

Liza ignored her, pointedly.

"Tell them," Shay urged before biting into one of the delicious buttered rolls.

"What?" Ro queried, looking from Shay to Liza and back again.

Liza slowly explained Shay's idea for harvesting Meadows South. As she talked, she could gauge the level of excitement that rose in the two women as their eyes widened and they leaned forward, meal forgotten.

Shay chuckled, filling with her own excitement to see that the idea was so well received.

"Oh, no way," Rosemary sighed. She looked at her partner and they shared a huge grin.

"Liza, Shay, you guys have hit on a fantastic idea," Kim said.

"Now, we can only pay minimum," Liza cautioned, shifting Stevie's sprawling weight on her lap. Having lost interest in her meal, Stevie had inserted her thumb into her mouth and was contentedly leaning back against her aunt's chest.

"More than enough for these folk." Ro brushed the issue aside. "I know ten right off the bat who would love this kind of work. You know, some of these older guys were made homeless by government cutbacks in farming."

Liza managed to take a bite. She covered her mouth and spoke around the food. "I know. George and I had a hell of a conversation one day. He used to own an acre and a half of land, grew tomatoes for contract."

Stevie wriggled down and ran across the patio toward Chloe and Scott just as a car sounded in the lot out front. By leaning far to one side, Liza alone could see Rich hurry outside via the front doorway and welcome the new arrival with a lingering hug and a look of fondness. She stopped chewing suddenly, the bite in her mouth turning to wood. It was CM. She sat back abruptly.

"Liza?" Shay asked. "What is it?"

Liza looked at the tablecloth and swallowed with some difficulty. "Omigosh, I should have guessed," she whispered.

Kim studied Liza. "Are you okay, Liza? What's wrong? Who was it?"

Liza glanced up, eyes distant. "No one. Just CM."

Ro frowned. "CM? He's never been here before. Did you invite him?"

"I...I think Rich did," Liza answered.

"That makes sense," Kim said, nodding and cutting turkey into small pieces. "They've gotten close, working together so long."

Liza smiled finally and her bemused gaze met Shay's worried eyes. "Yeah, guess so."

Later, when Rich and CM came, bearing laden plates, into the backyard to sit together on the low rock wall that bordered the gravel drive, Liza greeted CM warmly, a new sense of love for Rich swelling her heart. He would be fine.

CHAPTER FORTY-TWO

By nine that evening the guests and family had all cleared out, the food had been put away and the dishes washed. Shay could not stifle her yawns, some, no doubt, caused by the over-the-counter pain medicines she'd required to get through the day. Liza noticed and knew they needed to leave soon.

"We need to get you home," she said, gently rubbing Shay's back as they stood in the kitchen.

"I have my car here, remember? We went shopping in your truck. Do you need me to take Rosaries home?"

Liza smiled wickedly. "I'll take her. I thought I might come over for a while. That is, if you're not too tired."

Shay returned the smile, her forefinger tracing a seductive line along Liza's jaw. "Never too tired for you. Never."

Liza's eyes gleamed as she turned away, pulling Shay with her. Moving into the living room, they found *Mémé* and her father sitting together companionably. Not talking, just resting and staring at the droning television. Liza plopped down next to Rosaries and pulled Shay down next to her. "So where was Rich going?"

"Said he had to help CM with some bookkeeping," Tom answered absently.

"Ahh," Liza said, nodding her understanding. She patted Rosaries on the knee. "You about ready to go home, *Mémé?*"

"I am," Rosaries replied, but for a long time no one made a move, savoring the quality time together as a family. Another twenty minutes of football wrap-up passed before Rosaries rose with a sigh.

"Thanks, Rose, for everything," Tom said, rising to see her to the door. "You're welcome to stay another night, you know that."

Rosaries hugged Tom close. "*Oui*, you have always made an old woman feel welcome. I have things to tend to, my house she gets lonely, but I will be back at *Noel* and will stay again."

Liza loaded both bags into the bed of her truck, helped Rosaries in, waited patiently while Shay pulled the VW out of the drive, then pulled out after her.

"Did you have fun?" Liza asked.

Rosaries, her pocketbook held demurely in her lap, nodded. "I did. The family grows when we fall in love."

"Very true," Liza agreed. "What did you think of Chloe's fellow?"

"He is starched, I think," Rosaries replied, a forefinger smoothing one brow.

"Starched?" Liza frowned in the darkness. "You mean like stiff? I thought so too."

"I like Rich's man. He seems very nice. He is fat, but nice."

Liza chuckled. "So you think CM is Rich's beau, *Mémé?* I think you're right. I never thought Rich would like a man."

Rosaries shrugged. "It is love."

"*Oui, c'est amour,*" Liza teased as she pulled in front of Placide's Place. She helped Rosaries from the truck, carried her bag upstairs and made sure she was well settled, then made her way next door to Shay's.

The front porch was deserted and Liza felt a sudden worry

that her carefully laid plans had gone awry. As she mounted the porch however, the locks on the door slapped open and Shay was in her arms, a nervous Peaches lurking in the background.

"Oh, you sweet, sweet woman! How did you know about her? Who told you? I know I didn't tell you. Did you really do it? Adopt her for me? I thought you weren't allowed to do that, but I guess since everyone knew I loved her that made it okay. Isn't she beautiful, and she's got the sweetest personality." She paused for breath as she pulled Liza inside and reengaged the deadbolts. "I saw her out there and it terrified me, because I just saw a shadow in the headlights. Then she stepped forward and I saw it was her. She was tied to the railing with a big red bow around her neck and someone had put a bowl of water and an open bag of your food out there."

She took another deep breath and let silence fall. Peaches sat on the floor at Shay's feet, and Liza just watched them, speechless in the radiance of Shay's joy.

"I take it you like having her here?" she said finally.

Shay was grinning from ear to ear, her right hand absently fondling the dog's velvet ears. She nodded. "Words can't begin to...thank you, Liza."

Liza saw a new side to Shay then, a complete side. She sighed, gazing into the content, happy eyes of her lover. "You're welcome."

"You must be exhausted. I know I am," Shay said suddenly. "Do you think she needs to go out again? I say we just go to bed and she'll get us up if she needs to go. I know I should probably buy a crate and crate her at night, but I've never been very good at that. I *like* to sleep with dogs and feel alone when they're in their own bed. Crazy, I know, but I was always that way even as a little girl..."

Grinning and rolling her eyes, Liza followed Shay and Peaches into the bedroom, switching off lights as she encountered them.

Later, as the three of them lay quietly on the bed, Liza traced an index finger along the blue lizard inked into Shay's lower abdomen. It glowed with a purplish iridescence in the pale light streaming from the bathroom.

"Tell me about this," Liza cajoled gently.

Shay sighed and opened her eyes, one hand splayed across Peaches' soft back. "We have matching ones, Pepper and I. She insisted. One of her friends was a tattoo artist and we had them done together. It hurt like hell too and she said I was a baby for crying out. She didn't make one sound when she got hers, just puffed on a cigarette and read the newspaper. They're like mirror images of each other. She said when we stood together belly to belly it made a whole blue gecko."

"You hate it too, don't you?" Liza murmured.

"I do. One day I'll start having it removed. I've heard that's even more painful, and expensive. As much as I hate it, I just haven't been ready for that, I guess."

Liza leaned over and gently pressed a lingering kiss dead center on the lizard's torso. "I love it. You know why?" She looked up at Shay.

Shay brushed Liza's hair back. "Why, honey?"

"Because it's part of you now. No matter where it came from, it's yours and you can own it."

Shay smiled. "Come up here and hold me, you crazy gardener."

Liza moved to turn them into a spooning position.

"Wait!" Shay cried. "Don't disturb Peaches."

Liza laughed and shook her head from side to side. This was going to be interesting.

CHAPTER FORTY-THREE

"Isn't she just the prettiest thing?" Shay stated the next morning. Peaches was daintily eating from one of Shay's china soup bowls. "We've got to go shopping and get her some things of her own."

They sat at the kitchen table, early morning sunlight bathing the kitchen in a mellow mushroom of color. Peaches ate near Shay's feet and both women had their attention focused on the new addition.

"A little...different, maybe, but pretty? I dunno..." Liza sipped her coffee and pressed the warm cup to her cheek. They'd had a surprisingly uninterrupted night, but Peaches was starting to fidget. She had finished her food and was eyeing the two women expectantly.

"I guess we'd better take her out," Shay said, standing and

slipping her feet back into her slippers and retying the belt of her robe. She attached the lead to the dog's collar. "Let's take her down below so we can check out the area for the kennels."

Liza agreed and, carrying her coffee, followed Peaches and Shay out through the mudroom door. Both women looked toward Rosaries' house, toward the high veranda, but she wasn't out there. No doubt sleeping late, needing to rest from the hectic activity of the past two days. Peaches' tail wagged her svelte body with renewed glee when she finished relieving herself and came back close to Shay's side.

"So I thought I'd orient the buildings this way," Shay said, using her arms to manifest her vision for Liza. She went on to describe the novel way she wanted it constructed, even adding the possibility of focusing on the lemon yellow color she had envisioned earlier.

"I want the outside runs to have vinyl floors because they're healthier, but I think I still want concrete underneath so there'll be less shifting and fewer bugs."

Liza nodded. "How many kennels would you build?"

Shay paused thoughtfully, an index finger pressed to her lips. "Well, since it's mostly a dog *sitting* service, I don't want to just shove the babies off into kennels. I want to interact with them, you know?" She turned to Liza, seeking understanding. "I want to have dog-friendly common rooms, like a house, with doors and rooms but with lots of room to exercise."

"You could build it like a long barn," Liza said excitedly. "Like horse stalls with lots of common rooms. Maybe even get away from chain-link fencing."

Shay smiled and smoothed Peaches' coat. "Right! And we could have the whole building enclosed so there would be a long play and run area in between the stalls. That way all the dogs could visit even if they are separated by wooden fencing."

"I don't know," Liza said doubtfully. "What about fighting? The shelter keeps walls between their kennels."

Peaches left their side, moving toward the woods. She looked back toward the house.

Shay nodded, her mouth firm. "Dogs are territorial, true. But they can be taught to accept certain other dogs on their turf.

We had to train for that in the dog competitions because they're often crowded into the same room. It's pretty standard. There are usually some that just can't relax, though, even with training, and those we would have to separate off into their own rooms."

They fell silent, listening to mockingbirds calling to one another. A squirrel, or perhaps a chipmunk, scurried through the leafy undergrowth nearby. Peaches' ears perked and she turned toward it, chuffing a warning.

"I like the idea of caring for the dogs in a group. I'll have to make sure they are all up to date on their shots and just watch out for belligerent behavior," she added. She chewed a thumbnail as she surveyed the lay of the backyard.

Liza watched Shay, admiration and gentle love shining in her dark eyes.

"I think that would be perfect," she said softly. "And when it's all built, you could put an ad in the local fish wrap, and we could get Arlie to make you a nice wooden sign to put at the end of the drive. She's so good with that kind of stuff."

They discussed what materials Shay would use, leaning toward treated pine with an animal safe stain.

"You can get Al Jonas, from over at the sawmill, to help design and build it," Liza offered. "He's reasonable and might cut you a deal because he's a real animal lover."

Shay brightened considerably, dispelling her thoughtful mood. "That would be so great! I love what he did with the shelter. Do you think he would take the time to do it?"

"Why not? I'm sure of it," Liza replied. "Isn't it great to have something new to work on?"

"It really is," Shay agreed. "And it's exactly what I need now that I'm trying to let go of all this Pepper crap."

Liza laughed, causing Peaches to come closer, tail wagging, to see what all the fun was about. "Pepper crap? What a picture that evokes!"

Shay blushed and, seeing it, Liza laid an arm across her shoulders, pulling her closer. "Seriously, I am so glad to see you getting your life back. It's the greatest thing of all."

They kissed gently, then, hand in hand, spent a good while walking around the yard and enjoying the cool Alabama morning.

Later, refreshed, still eagerly discussing the new project, they walked back into the house through the mudroom.

"I need to go," Liza said, placing her coffee cup in the kitchen sink. "I need to go home and put on the fancy duds so I can attend the annual board meeting at Meadows."

"Oh no." Shay was disappointed. "Is that today?"

Liza sighed. "Yep, and I dread it. I just like the gardening end of the company, not the business part. I am going to pitch the Meadows South idea today, though, so that's something."

"Have you talked to anyone about it?"

"I called the number cruncher after I got the idea from you, and he was all over it, loving the idea. He saw a lot of growth potential."

Shay smiled shyly and looked at Liza from beneath lowered lashes. "We're a pretty good team, aren't we?"

Liza pulled Shay close, cupping the back of her head into one firm hand. "Yes, we are, without a doubt," she said. She kissed Shay with gentle longing, then hurried to dress.

CHAPTER FORTY-FOUR

After waving goodbye to Liza and checking the locks, Shay made her way to the bedroom, realizing suddenly that Peaches wasn't by her side. Figuring she was dozing in a patch of sunlight somewhere, she went into the bedroom and gathered her clothes together preparatory to taking a shower. After just a few moments however, she missed the boxer's company and went looking for her.

She found her in the guest bedroom, sprawled next to the closet door, her nose pressed to the crack along the bottom. When Shay entered, Peaches whined and sat back on her haunches, looking at her expectantly.

"You just went out, sweetie and, besides, that's a closet. Can you wait just a little longer? I'm only half dressed now." She motioned for Peaches to follow her and the dog did, all the way into the bathroom.

After a quick shower, Shay stepped from the stall and playfully splashed water on the dog. Peaches licked water from

Shay's legs as she wrapped her hair in a fluffy towel and her body in her favorite thick terry robe. Peaches moved to wait patiently beside the door to the bedroom.

"You are such a good girl," Shay crooned as she rinsed her mouth and dabbed her face with sunblock. "Waiting for Mommy, so patiently. Let's go in the other room and after I'm dressed, we'll pop outside for another walk."

Peaches stood and shook her body as Shay opened the door. Shay stepped through and stopped abruptly when Peaches growled. A short, plump woman stood in the bedroom.

"Who are you?" Shay said, her voice trembling.

"Yeah, I know. I look a sight, don't I?" the woman said and Shay's heart plummeted in her chest until she couldn't catch a breath. She'd know that clipped British voice anywhere. Pepper.

"I'm gonna fix it though," the woman continued, indicating the plastic grocery bag held in her hand.

Shay was paralyzed and could not respond. Thoughts inundated her, however. The eyes watching her with such amusement were brown, not blue. The hair was long, unkempt, and graying in the front. The woman was also heavier than Pepper, by about forty pounds. How could Pepper's voice be coming from this woman's mouth?

Shay tried to speak, only to discover her mouth filled with cotton. Trying again, she moistened her tongue and pressed one hand over her rapidly thumping heart. "Who...who are you?"

The woman looked heavenward. "How quickly they forget."

She moved toward Shay with astonishing speed and grabbed the collar of her robe, pulling her face close. "You bitch," she snarled. "How dare you presume to forget me, after I rotted in that prison, thanks to you."

Shay saw it then. It was her, disguised somehow but definitely Pepper.

"Pepper," Shay stammered. "How...how did you find me?"

Pepper released her, as if satisfied that Shay's memory had returned.

"That prissy shrink," she replied, looking around the bedroom possessively.

"You killed her, didn't you?" Shay's mind felt numb. One thought did penetrate, however, and that was relief that Pepper no longer had the sensual hold on her that she'd had in the past.

"Her fault. If she'd left me alone..." She shrugged and placed the bag on Shay's bureau.

"But...how did you get in here?"

"I knew you'd have to take the damned mutt out at some point. I just waited until the door was unlocked." She smiled a strange gap-toothed smile that was foreign to Shay. "You and that Amazon were down the hill and never even saw me."

"But..." Shay tried to wrap her mind around this. After all her precautions, it had been that easy.

"Okay, enough of this foolishness. You still belong to me and don't you forget it."

With lightning speed, one thick arm wrapped around Shay's neck, knocking the towel askew. Pepper ripped the towel off, dropped it to the floor, and then mussed Shay's long, wet tresses, entangling her hand in them.

Shay cried out but was powerless to prevent Pepper from dragging her to the bed. Pepper pushed Shay down and jumped to sit on top of her. Taking her time, avoiding Shay's battling limbs, Pepper deftly looped and tied scarves around each of her wrists, then fastened them securely to the bedposts. She moved off and stood back as if admiring her handiwork. She had not bothered to tie the feet and Shay bucked, kicking, eyes wide in terror, a strange huffing gurgle coming from her throat.

Peaches, who had been watching them and wagging her tail playfully, suddenly became antsy, sidestepping and whining quietly. She licked her chops and looked from one woman to the other.

"Now, you stay there a minute," Pepper said absently. She moved toward the bathroom, lifting the bag from the bureau. "I've got some great plans for us. I kind of like it here and this house is perfect. Good choice."

Shay could hear water running in the sink. Though still numb with shock, she realized she needed to escape *now*, so she writhed against the scarves, trying to loosen the knots Pepper had tied.

"What made you pick this town?" Pepper continued conversationally. "I heard what y'all were talking about. We could do well, being in business here. One thing I learned at that damned shelter. People in the South love their bloody canines. They'd pay big to have somebody babysit them."

Shay could hear strange sounds that she couldn't identify. Peaches came to the bed and laid her muzzle on the mattress, looking at Shay with confused brown eyes. Shay looked back, sorrow filling her as she thought of what Pepper might do to her new friend.

"I'm so, so sorry," she whispered to the dog, tears cascading from the corners of her eyes and down along her cheeks.

"What's that?" Pepper stuck her head around the door and peered at Shay. She had cropped half her hair close to her head while the other half still hung long. She looked comical, if only Shay could have found levity in this moment. Pepper disappeared again, but her voice floated out to the bedroom.

"Since we like it here, maybe we could start training dogs again too. I see you got the new mutt. The minute I laid eyes on her, I knew you'd go apeshit over her. I was the one who put her in Carol's office that day. I wanted to make sure you saw her."

Shay stilled suddenly. How long had Pepper been here? "I...I don't understand. What are you talking about?"

Pepper laughed. "Oh yeah, I been watching and waiting. You know I'm the soul of patience, as you like to say."

"But...but," Shay began, staring at the bathroom door. "How could you? I was there."

Pepper's voice became angry and Shay quaked inside. "Get a grip, Virginia Faith! No one notices people working in the background. I learned that real quick in prison after getting beaten up a few times and having my teeth knocked out. Stay in the background and wait til the time is right. Good lesson."

Pepper appeared suddenly and Shay gasped. The transformation was remarkable. The brown eyes, obviously contacts, were gone, the bright blue had returned and the hair, as short as Shay remembered it, no longer shone bright blond but the gray lent a similar lightness to it. It *was* Pepper. She was heavier and missing a few teeth, with a new, jagged scar above her left eyebrow, but it was unmistakably her.

"I hate you!" Shay blurted without thinking. "You're a monster! I hate what you did and I hate who you are. Why can't you just go away and leave me alone?"

Pepper stared at her a long moment, eyes turning steely. With a growl, she pounced on Shay and curled her hand around the front of Shay's neck. She squeezed, choking the smaller woman.

"You...are...*such*...a...*bitch*," she ground out. "I come all the way down here just because I still, *still* fucking love you, and you have the nerve to talk to me like that."

Peaches growled low in her throat, and Shay felt new alarm stir. *Oh, God, please be quiet, sweet baby, oh, Jesus, please don't make her notice you,* Shay's mind shrieked.

Pepper swung her head around and eyed the dog, easing her grip on Shay. Shay took a deep, shuddering breath, filling her burning lungs as Pepper moved clumsily from the bed.

"You, Miss *Thang*, need to go outside, don't you?" Her tone was gentle, wheedling, and Peaches responded, seeming to hope sincerely she was wrong in thinking that this woman who'd been caring for her was going to hurt her new mommy. She bowed her front and joyfully wagged her tail, seeking favor.

"Don't you hurt her," Shay croaked as loudly as her tortured throat would allow. "I will kill you myself."

Pepper eyed her doubtfully. "Right," she said, her voice heavily sarcastic.

"Come on," Pepper cooed to the dog, striding into the living room and unlocking the front door. Using her foot, she pushed the dog out and slammed the door hard before making her way back to the bedroom.

"Now, where were we?" she said, hands on hips.

When Pepper's eyes focused on her, Shay realized with horror that her frantic thrashing had loosened her robe and she might as well have been entirely naked. She realized that if Pepper touched her in that way, her psyche would shatter into a million irretrievable shards.

Pepper moved closer and traced one forefinger along Shay's ankle. Shay jerked the foot away. Undaunted, Pepper persisted, one palm sliding along Shay's calf, knee and up to her inner thigh. Shay moaned in horror and felt about as close to insanity as a person could be.

"That woman, that tall one? She's not our type, and I don't want nothing more to do with her, you hear me? You won't answer her calls, you won't let her in, and there'll be no more of this cheating on me. You know I won't allow that. I say when and I say how. Understand?"

Pepper's face was only inches from hers and Shay went away in her mind. She no longer saw Pepper but heard a strange far-away ringing sound that eventually stopped abruptly.

CHAPTER FORTY-FIVE

Liza actually jumped when the connection silenced with a harsh screech. Finally dressed and with a stack of copious notes on the seat beside her, she was barreling toward the interstate that would take her to Montgomery, worried that she wouldn't make the eleven o'clock meeting. Still, she wanted to hear Shay's voice and make plans for later that evening. Maybe they'd meet the others at CM's and lift a celebratory toast if her ideas for a Meadows South were well received by the entire board.

Glancing at the phone, she laughed, thinking Shay must have dropped the phone, or, true to form, let Peaches try to answer it, so she hit redial. A jarring tone sounded and a computerized voice came on, told her the client was unavailable and asked her to leave a message. Shay closed the phone and tapped it to her chin. Maybe Shay was talking to Don and didn't want to be interrupted. Liza sighed. That didn't feel right. Shay would ask Don to hold, pop on to explain and arrange to call back. Liza knew this because she had done it before.

Deciding to wait and see if she'd call back, Liza focused on the road ahead. The humidity was up so she'd switched on the air as soon as she got on the road. It wouldn't do for her to arrive at the board meeting puddled in sweat and windblown. She chuckled to herself. It wouldn't be the first time. She was a little nervous about seeing Gina again but felt confident that time would heal old wounds.

She waited a full five minutes by the dashboard clock. She tried the number and again it went right to voice mail. Liza felt a nibble of uncertainty. This was unusual; Shay had never ignored her calls. Ever. An uneasy feeling began to creep over her. She pondered it, chewing it into tastelessness with her mind, ideas attacking like persistent flies at a picnic. What was it?

She drove on, unable to pinpoint the cause of her unease.

CHAPTER FORTY-SIX

Pepper ground the broken cell phone under the heel of her athletic shoe and studied Shay. The redhead had closed her eyes and didn't appear to be breathing. Pepper walked close and prodded the bottom of her foot. She didn't move. Pepper circled the bed, admiring the long lean lines of Shay's half-naked torso. She saw bruises along Shay's outer thigh and wondered what the tall blond had done to her. What kind of games had *they* played? Shay loved it rough. She would never change. Whistling a merry tune, Pepper reentered the bathroom and began neatening the mess she'd made while cutting her hair. She could hear the damned dog barking outside and knew she'd have to deal with that soon.

Strangely enough, it was Uncle Stamos who came to Shay. His face bobbed into her mind, his fuzzy red hair as disordered as ever. He was dressed in torn, faded jeans and his Rolling Stones T-shirt had a rip through the red tongue part of the logo. Shay could see his pale chest through the gaping hole.

"Shay," he said calmly, eying her with washed-out blue eyes. "You're in a pickle."

"What should I do?" Shay asked worriedly. She felt a little dizzy because of the way she and Stamos were slowly revolving around one another.

"What do you want to do?" he asked, raising one thin, heavily freckled hand above his head in a type of wriggling dance.

Shay sighed and jutted one hip, forced into dancing with him in this strange halfway place. "I really want to be with El," she murmured.

He looked at her steadily, then winked. "Well, that answers that then, doesn't it?"

He disappeared.

"El," Shay said aloud, her mouth dry and swollen. "Liza."

She opened her eyes and discovered nothing had changed. She could hear Pepper in the next room, going through the cabinets and muttering to herself.

With new determination, trying to pull clear of the clouds of fear enervating her, Shay slowly worked her wrist against the restraint on her right arm. There had to be a way to work it loose. *Think, Shay*, she told herself angrily as she worked against the scarf. *You're no dummy.* Her eyes roamed the room looking for a Plan B.

"You might as well give it up," Pepper said. She stood in the doorway drying her hands on Shay's favorite decorative towel. Her eyes were bright and, to Shay, evil. The woman would eventually, someday, kill her.

Think, Shay, think. Remember something, anything.

"My hands are asleep," she said in her best little girl voice.

Pepper came close, immediately contrite. "Oh, I'm sorry, honey. I didn't mean to make them so tight."

She leaned in, untied the left one and looped it more loosely around Shay's wrist. Shay saw her chance and took it. She heaved her body to the right, slipping her left hand free and reaching for the right scarf. Magically, due to the angle of her twisting motion, her right hand pulled free and she ran toward the door, her white robe flapping like albino manta ray wings. Pepper, though momentarily caught off guard, quickly recovered and, with a shouted curse, took off after Shay.

CHAPTER FORTY-SEVEN

Liza was unhappy. The harder she tried not to focus on her worry about Shay, the more intense the worry became. She called repeatedly, hitting redial, hearing the mechanical voice mail robot and then immediately dialing again. Something was definitely wrong. There was no way she could blithely head off to Montgomery and focus on the meeting. Not until she heard Shay's voice. Making up her mind, she pulled over, out of the stream of traffic, and tried three more times, actually leaving messages until the phone told her the voice mailbox was full.

"That does it," she told herself grimly. She pulled back onto the interstate but took the next exit and headed back toward Maypearl.

She pressed another speed dial key and got her grandmother on the line.

"*Mémé*, I think there's something wrong. Where are you?"

"*Dans le salon. Pourquoi?*"

"Good. Can you run upstairs and look over toward Shay's and tell me what you see?"

"*Oui*, hold."

Liza heard the clatter of the house phone as it hit the end table, then silence. She tapped her index finger on the steering wheel as she waited.

"A dog, it is out of doors barking," Rosaries said urgently when she returned. "There is nothing else."

"Can you see Shay? Is she out there with the dog?"

"*Non*, and the dog it looks upset. Where is this dog come from?"

"I had Chris bring it over yesterday, a present for Shay," Liza answered absently. Shay would never have left Peaches outside alone. Not the way she babied that dog.

"Chris? Who is this Chris?" Rosaries asked.

"She's just a homeless gal who works..." A sudden light flashed and Liza's stomach plummeted. She suddenly felt sick and thought she might vomit. A series of images flashed through her mind. She saw Chris, she saw the photo of Pepper and she saw the tip of a purple tail peeking from the top of Chris's jeans as she helped load crates of recycling onto the back of Liza's truck.

"Aww, fuck," she whispered.

"Liza, *écoutez!* You want me to go find Shay?"

"No, *Mémé*, I'm calling the sheriff. Don't go over there, it's dangerous, okay?"

Liza slammed the phone shut and hot tears coursed along her cheeks. How could she have been so damned stupid? Pepper, the conniving bitch, had played all of them. She realized suddenly that she had never seen Christine and Shay in the same room. Chris had mysteriously disappeared the day they worked the dogs, and she'd also been absent at each Thanksgiving dinner at the shelter.

She flipped open the phone, dialed 911 and increased her speed. If anything happened to Shay, it would be her fault. She had led Pepper right to Shay's door.

CHAPTER FORTY-EIGHT

Racing into the living room, Shay panicked, uncertain where to go to escape the woman barreling along behind her. As if lit by divine light, she saw that the front door locks hadn't been engaged; she made a beeline for the door. She grasped the doorknob just as Pepper's hand entangled in the back of her robe.

The door flew open and Shay whirled, kicking out at Pepper. The older woman anticipated the move and easily sidestepped the kick. Luckily, she had grabbed only a fistful of the belt sewn to the back of the robe. It pulled loose with a loud rip, and Shay fell through the door and onto the floorboards of the porch, hitting squarely on the bruised area hurt when she'd fallen in the grocery store. The pain made her head swim but in survival mode, she began scooting along the porch, splinters digging into her palms and flanks. Pepper grabbed a handful of Shay's hair and jerked her to her knees.

A sudden stream of angry French sounded, and Shay twisted around to see Liza's grandmother rapidly approaching, a baseball bat lifted high above her head and Peaches at her side. Shay swung around to look at Pepper and saw a look she would remember for a long time. She wanted to laugh but could not spare the time. Taking advantage of Pepper's surprise, she pulled loose and, rising, shoved her body against Pepper, knocking the woman off balance. Shay lost some hair in the exchange but considered it a fair trade. Pepper tumbled backward, falling off the elevated porch and landing with a jarring thump on the lawn. Peaches circled her, growling and barking, and Rosaries stood over Pepper threatening her with the bat and shouting at her in French. Shay pulled her robe tightly about herself and sank to the porch steps, a palm pressed to her chest trying to calm her racing heart.

The peace was short-lived however. Pepper, with a snarl, leapt to her feet and took a swing at Rosaries. Gasping in horror, Shay rose to go to the elderly woman's aid but was gratified to see Rosaries dodge the blow and swing the bat which connected hard on Pepper's left shoulder. Pepper howled and reacted, going after the old woman, grabbing at her hair with her uninjured right arm and trying to use leverage to take Rosaries down. Shay and Peaches both leapt on Pepper at the same time. Peaches sank her wide jaws into Pepper's right calf, and Pepper screamed as the bone was pressed. Shay tried to push her off balance and Rosaries, finally freed, reached for the fallen bat as welcome sirens sounded in the distance.

Seeing that she might be outfought, Pepper shook off the dog and decided to run. She vaulted across the short fence that marked the boundaries of Shay's lawn and took off limping through the woods. Peaches raced after her as Rosaries gathered Shay into her arms.

CHAPTER FORTY-NINE

Liza made a scorching, dangerous turn onto Shay's driveway from the asphalt of Dooley Drive and saw a figure stumbling through the wooded area below Shay's house. It looked like a small man, but Liza knew it had to be Pepper. Braking in a cloud of dust and gravel, Liza leapt from her truck and took off after her.

Hampered by her tucked-in shirt, she pulled it loose, wishing desperately that she had something on other than tight trousers and dress shoes. It seemed she'd never catch her.

Seeing the color blue blooming through the trees, Liza realized Pepper had parked her blue pickup truck at the base of the forest, well hidden from the house. Anger clenched in Liza's chest when she heard the engine roar to life. She raced headlong down the hill, her flesh tearing on brambles and her feet twisting on roots. She made it to the truck just in time to swing herself up and onto the pickup bed as Pepper guided the wheels toward the road. Liza reached through the open back windshield and grabbed a handful of Pepper's shirt.

"You're not going anywhere!" she cried.

Pepper, not realizing Liza had given chase nor gained the bed of the truck, turned and looked at her, eyes wide with surprise. Liza realized that, with blue eyes and closely cropped hair, she looked nothing like Christine. At that same moment, Peaches made a jump for the open passenger window, scrambling for purchase but finally making it inside. Pepper screamed in terror and wildly stomped the gas pedal. The truck leapt forward, fairly flying across Dooley, then the wide dirt shoulder and finally breaking through the calm surface of Dooley's Folly.

When the truck hit the water, the impact twisted Liza and she felt a bone in her right arm snap. Howling with pain, she let go of Pepper and pulled the arm close, even as she tumbled backward off the truck and into the water. As the water closed over her head, she moved her broken arm and almost drowned trying to cry out from the pain. Using her left arm, she managed to surface and saw Pepper in the driver's seat of the rapidly sinking truck. She'd hit her head against the steering wheel and blood coursed in a ghastly stream down her face. She was struggling to open the door, which had been crushed as it scraped a tree on its way through the woods.

Gritting her teeth against the pain, Liza found footing in the shallows around the back of the truck and stepped into the depths again to try to get the dog and Pepper out of the passenger side of the truck before it went down. Gasping from the pain of moving her arm, she inhaled water and coughed the entire way as she made her way to the passenger window.

She couldn't get the door open against the pressure of the water, especially with only one arm. She hooked her left hand in Peaches' collar and helped pull her through the window, going under in the process. Resurfacing, she braced her good armpit on the window ledge as the red and blue lights from the screaming police cruisers flashed across her.

"Come on," she cried, motioning for Pepper to come through the window. "The truck's going down."

Pepper sat very still, as though the situation weren't critical. She turned her bloody face toward Liza, staring at her with cold, hateful blue eyes. Surrounded by the streaming blood, the eyes were downright grisly. Liza looked away but continued to reach for Pepper until she felt the woman slap her helping hand away. Glancing back, she saw that the encroaching pond water had reached up to Pepper's chin. Pepper didn't seem to be worried; she simply relaxed further against the backrest, allowing the water to close over her.

When Peaches' dog-paddling paws grazed Liza's broken arm, bringing tears to her eyes, she released herself from the truck and pulled the dog to shallower water. She reclined there panting, Peaches licking her face, as she watched the truck go down in a swirling whirlpool.

CHAPTER FIFTY

"She had a bad, bad childhood," Shay said softly. "Had brothers and a father who were pretty mean to her."

A breeze snuck in and lifted a tendril of her unbound ruddy hair. The teasing caress lingered, then ceased abruptly. Peaches, panting lightly, pressed against Shay's leg and she bent absently to caress the long, fuzzy ears.

The three stood together at the northern edge of Dooley's Folly. The peaceful water showed none of the trauma from yesterday's events, except in its disturbed, murky undertones. The salvage crew had come earlier that morning and removed the truck wreckage. The only evidence that something tragic had occurred here could be found in the flattened, muddy foliage and skid marks embedded in the dirt banks.

Pepper's body had been recovered after the accident, and

both women felt an enormous sense of guilty relief that the threat of her had been taken from their lives. It was sad that Pepper had chosen death to future incarceration, but Shay, who had known her best, was not surprised.

Liza shifted her weight from one foot to the other, eyes never leaving the water. She was groggy from the pain medication the hospital had given her. "It's no excuse. There is no excuse for what she did to you."

Shay sighed heavily. "I know. And she was Chris, from the shelter, the homeless woman who lived at the mission?"

"Yes. I had no clue. I feel like such a fool... She had this all planned out, even traveling with a man."

Liza had been relieved that Shay understood her earlier apology about unknowingly leading Pepper to her, but guilt lingered.

"There's no way you could have known, honey. No way. I didn't even recognize her."

Liza stirred impatiently. "But still, she was new to the area. That should have set off alarm bells, but here I was, working right alongside the enemy, for Pete's sake."

Shay laid a calming hand on Liza's shoulder. "It happened and it's over. Let it go. I'm not sorry she's gone. I have to say that."

Liza studied Shay, eyes fixing on the bright white bandages that peppered her lover's face and arms. "Me too, honey. No matter what, we would have always had that fear in the back of our minds. That she was out there somewhere and could harm us. Yet again."

Shay smiled hesitantly, catching and connecting Liza's gaze. "Us? Have we become an us, you and me?"

Liza pulled Shay close with her good arm, her gaze holding Shay captive. "You know I wouldn't have it any other way."

Peaches insinuated her body between the two, tail wagging and slamming against their legs. She appeared to have recovered completely from the trauma of the day before, having been left with only a small gash on one flank. Both women laughed at her intrusion. Shay took Liza's hand.

"Come to the house?" The request was coy and unbearably enticing to Liza. "I'll put an ice pack on your cast."

"I bet you will," Liza said pointedly.

Shay laughed lightly and her voice grew soft. "You know I'll always take care of you, don't you?"

"Yes, and you know I'll always take care of you, right?"

Shay nodded and leaned up for a quick kiss. Their eyes met, gazes lingering.

"Lead the way, sweetheart, and I'll follow," Liza said, her voice low and full of promise.